Prometheus for Breakfast

Jack Tilde

Dover Sole
Publishing

Library of Congress Control Number: 2025930205

ISBN: 979-8-9922224-0-1

To my father, who taught me how to turn pain into laughter, and to my wife and children, who made sure I rarely needed to.

Prometheus for Breakfast

A Novel by Jack Tilde

Chapter 1
The DMV

The end of the world could have been avoided if only Ms. November had held lemons, but that's entropy for you.

To understand the profound nature of this statement, we must start with the story of Richard Wilkins—an exceptionally unexceptional man of average height and weight, middle-aged, and exactly a five on the standard one-to-ten scale of attractiveness based on the opinions of the opposite sex and a small number of the same sex who had given his appearance any consideration at all.

He and his wife of more than twenty years, Clara, had two unremarkable children and lived in a modest beige box of a home in a small midwestern town whose name is not worth divulging both because it's too dull to dedicate any time to and, even if I give the name, there's a 99.98% probability you haven't heard of it.

A loyal husband, Richard shared with his wife an affection that, like most monogamous relationships between *Homo sapiens*, was primarily based on a lack of other suitable options given the geographic remoteness of the area in which they'd

1

met and the societal expectation that Clara hurry up and wed before she was no longer biologically capable of procreating. A phenomenon that most cultures give the title "true love."

Aside from his devotion to his family, the only thing even modestly notable about Richard was his curious mind—a trait that both defined him and frequently left him feeling alienated from the stifling orthodoxy of the town in which he was born and raised, and, for the sake of our story, has died . . .

———

I n a pitch-black hallway with a faint glimmer of light at the end, these were the first words Richard heard: "Please, move toward the light."

The voice was feminine yet robotic. "Please, move toward the light. Please, move toward the light."

As Richard headed toward the light, he picked up more voices in the distance. Some spoke in English, and others spoke in languages he couldn't understand. But he continued toward the light in hopes he could figure out where he was and what was happening.

He felt a lump in the back of his throat, and his heart was beating rapidly—the result of a fight-or-flight instinct sent into overdrive that left his hands shaky and thoughts unclear.

As he reached the source of the light, the darkness gave way to a single incandescent light bulb positioned above a gray door with the letters *DMV* stenciled on it in black.

DMV? Richard thought. *Department of Motor Vehicles? Huh? Why am I here? I just renewed my license last spring.*

Because it seemed a better option than heading back down the hallway into the unknown darkness, Richard opened the door and went inside.

On the other side of the door was a room that resembled

every DMV Richard had ever visited. Rows of blue plastic chairs with shiny metal legs. Walls lined with numbered windows protecting a back area filled with small cubicles. An overwhelming sense of grayness that was only made more depressing by the rows of dour faces both in the blue chairs and behind the service windows.

"Now serving number two-four-seven-two at window number nine," blared over the intercom.

Richard stepped forward and noticed a red device protruding from the wall with a numbered ticket sticking out and the words *Take One* on a placard above it. He took a number and found a seat among the ocean of plastic chairs.

As Richard took his seat, he glanced at his ticket.

Number two-four-seven-eight. That won't be a bad wait at all.

For hours, Richard scanned the room in hopes of finding answers but only found more questions.

Why is there a woman in a bathing suit sitting next to a man in a parka? And who wears a bathing suit to the DMV?

Why does everyone wearing a business suit look so worried? And why does that man with a flag pin on his lapel look more worried than the others?

Why is there a naked old man in a shower cap at the DMV? And why doesn't he seem the least bit ashamed?

"Now serving number two-four-seven-eight at window number eighteen," someone said in a robotic voice over the intercom.

Jolted from his thoughts, Richard leapt from his seat and rushed toward window eighteen.

The rotund clerk working the window wore an orange blouse that made her look like an enormous tangerine. She had curly brown hair, glasses, and a tired face that made Richard anxious before he reached the window. A brown nameplate at the front of her desk read *Janet*, which any reasonable person would have safely assumed was her name.

"Hi, Janet," Richard said, as he placed two shaky hands on her counter and produced a plastic smile. "I-I believe there must be some mistake. I'm not sure why I'm here. I don't know how to get out. But if you can point me in the direction of an exit that doesn't lead into an endless dark hallway, I'll happily be out of your hair."

Janet rolled her eyes and began speaking in a monotone-yet-annoyed fashion, as if she had uttered the words a million times before. "Welcome to the Department of Mortal Vacation. My name's Janet. You're dead. It's my job to assign you an eval-uator to help determine where you go from here. Please be patient as I review your file."

"Vacation?" Richard asked, the word taking an unexpected twist in the context of the afterlife.

Janet rolled her eyes again. "Yes. Vacation. A word meaning the end of work. The start of a break from something. In this case, the end of your life. The throwing off of your mortal coil." She paused and peered over the top of her glasses with piercing judgment. "And no, not a vacation to the Bahamas." She began shuffling through Richard's file. "Your evaluator will be Peter. He's in office 386C. Take this file up the stairs behind me, up to the third floor, and hang a left. It's the 86th door on your right. If you fall into a bottomless abyss, you've gone too far."

"Thank you," Richard replied to the burnt-out bureaucrat as he gathered his paperwork. "I think."

Humans espouse many beliefs about what happens when we die. The most common faiths preach that we go to an afterlife that is either wonderful or awful, depending on factors such as how we behaved in life, how we performed certain dances, or what family we were born into. Other faiths believe we are reincarnated in a kind of cosmic soul-recycling system, repeating an endless pattern of life and death until we learn from our past mistakes and reach a state of enlightenment that frees us from our mortal struggles. But from what we can ascertain about our ability to learn from our mistakes, it's doubtful this happens with any sort of regularity.

The strangest of these is likely the belief held by the inhabitants of the small island nation of Babadooshuru, where the locals believe that all of reality takes place in the body of a giant self-eating snake and that when they die, they're shat out through the snake's anus back into its mouth to experience reality anew. To celebrate this renewal, the believers of this faith often bless each other by rubbing snake feces in the eyes of their fellow congregants. This act, though seemingly barbaric, is still more humane than the way followers of Western religion have historically treated one another.

Amazingly, none of these belief systems has gotten it quite right . . .

After almost an hour of panicked fumbling through the stairways and hallways of the DMV, Richard found room 386C on the left side of the hallway in a wing of the building separate from the one Janet had described, but he, like most deceased souls, was in no position to go back and correct her. Thus, he could only conclude she would likely continue to give bad directions to every soul that approached her desk from now until eternity.

As he approached Peter's office, he found the door open and Peter sitting at his desk shuffling paperwork. Peter was a scrawny man in glasses, with blond bowl-cut hair, gray slacks, and a long-sleeved yellowing dress shirt that was about two sizes too big for his thin frame.

"Hi. Um, are you Peter?"

"You're late," Peter said, without looking up from the pile of manilla folders and documents stacked atop his desk. "People who respect my time aren't late."

Richard stepped into Peter's cluttered little office and glanced at several messy file cabinets and a cart holding a boxy old television with a VCR atop it. "Sorry, it's just . . . Janet downstairs told me you'd be the eighty-sixth door on the right on the third floor. I walked all the way to the edge of the abyss before backtracking and finding you."

"Janet, huh?" Peter said, with narrow eyes and a slight frown.

"Yes. Janet. Large woman. Glasses. Orange dress."

Peter dropped the act and began to laugh. "That's Janet! She's such a hoot!"

"A hoot?"

"Yeah, she loves to give people bad directions just to make them sweat! Life of the party, that gal!"

Richard wondered if they were talking about the same Janet. After a brief pause, he took a seat across the desk from Peter.

"So, I'm Peter, but you know that already. I'm sure Janet already informed you that you're dead."

"Yes, she did," Richard replied, feeling a mix of disbelief and resignation as he tried to process the absurdity of his situation.

"Wonderful." Peter broke eye contact and began sorting through Richard's paperwork. "So it's my job to evaluate your file and decide if you belong in Heaven or Hell. Think of me kind of like an insurance adjuster. I review your case, adjust the good and the bad, and decide where you belong."

Richard was struck by a sense of familiarity: a man named Peter would decide if he was worthy of Heaven or Hell. He would have been embarrassed to admit that he owed the memory more to random episodes of his favorite sitcoms than anything he had learned at church. "Wait. Are you Saint Peter? Like *the* Saint Peter?"

Peter glanced up from his paperwork with a sly smile. "Why, yes. Yes I am, my son." He raised his hands into the air and peered upward as if expecting the ceiling to open and the light of Heaven to shine down upon him. "I'm Saint Peter, who, according to legend, guards the gates of Heaven."

"Wow," Richard replied, surprised and slightly starstruck. "That . . . that's amazing. It's an honor to meet you. Honestly. Don't take this the wrong way, but I always pictured you taller and . . . beardier."

Peter slapped the mountain of paperwork on his desk and leaned back in his chair, howling with laughter. "Oh! I got you! I got you so good! You should have seen your face!"

Richard was now sufficiently confused.

"'Are you *the* Saint Peter?'" Peter repeated in a mocking tone. "Of course not! But I had you convinced for a minute! Do you think everyone who works here named Peter is *the* Saint Peter? That'd be like me assuming every Richard that walks in my door is Richard the Lionheart or Richard Simmons! Shoot, I'm not even the only Peter in this hallway. There are three more Peters between offices 316C and 392C. Funny enough, there's a guy named Jesus who works on this floor too, but obviously not *the* Jesus. That guy has all kinds of fun with his evaluees." He removed his glasses, wiped his eyes, and brought his laughter under control. "So, no. I'm Peter the nobody, and you aren't Richard Branson. You're Richard Wilkins, a nobody in every sense of the word."

Richard took offense but was too embarrassed to speak up. "That's a good one. You got me."

Peter adopted a more somber demeanor, both in tone and expression, no doubt hoping to salvage what was left of his professionalism. "Anyway, I'm sure you have a million more questions right now that probably aren't as absurd as your last one. Lucky for you, I'm required to show you a short orientation video that should answer all your questions while I review your paperwork."

Peter wheeled the TV cart closer to Richard and fiddled with the controls.

Static appeared on the screen. After a few seconds, '80s synth-pop began to radiate from the television speakers, sounding unmistakably like the beginning of Van Halen's hit song "Jump." On the television appeared a blue-and-purple gradient splash screen with the title *What Am I Doing Here?* and below that, the words *A Production of GOD.*

The tape was staticky, like it had been played a million times.

A star wiped across the screen, revealing an office with a man leaning against the front of a large wood desk. Slightly plump, with a white beard and shoulder-length white hair, he bore more resemblance to Jerry Garcia than Santa Claus—edgier and less jovial, but still nonthreatening. He wore a black suit and tie and a black pair of square-rimmed glasses. "Welcome," the man said. "My name's Joe, but you may know me as Jehovah."

Once again, Richard recognized the name. Unlike his memory of Saint Peter, the recollection didn't come from his

8

favorite sitcoms but from the name's eponymous witnesses that frequented his front door with pamphlets espousing the benefits of their particular brand of Christianity. The realization that he was looking at a man he could only assume was the Judeo-Christian God sent a tingling pulse of electricity down his spine and into his arms and legs.

"If you're watching this video, you're dead. Congratulations on the completion of your simulation period." Joe spoke in a stiff tone and cadence that made it clear he was reading from a cue card. "An exciting new adventure awaits you here in the afterlife. But before we can talk about what's next, let's talk about how we got here."

A star once again wiped across the screen, presenting a rolling collage of corporate stock photos. There was the usual group of smiling people sitting around a table in a boardroom photo. The photo of a man in front of a computer screen raising his arms in an expression of victory. The woman in a blazer, smiling, arms confidently crossed over her chest. And, of course, the photo of a man enthusiastically pointing to a meaningless jumble of random numbers on a whiteboard.

Joe continued to narrate in the background as the collage rotated through the images. "The office you're in is part of General Observable Dimension Inc.—GOD for short—a company formed by the merger of Observable Dimension One Inc. and Aesthetic Observable Dimension LLC. I'm the founder and CEO of GOD, and we created everything you perceived as reality."

Richard was speechless, his mind racing. *God is a corporation? How is that possible?*

"I know what you're thinking," Joe continued. "'GOD is a corporation? And, if so, what kind of business?'"

Richard began to believe no thought could cross his mind

that hadn't crossed the minds of millions of others who had sat in the same chair.

"Your universe, your entire reality was once a dimension that existed as a void. We took that void and installed a physical simulation designed by the talented engineers and creators at GOD to help us better understand ourselves and the meaning behind our existence. We made you in our likeness to learn from your mistakes before we make them ourselves so we can model our society around the best of yours. In working to perfect your species, GOD helps us to perfect our own."

The image on the screen changed to a flowchart that featured several large bags with dollar signs on them. Arrows from the bags all pointed to the word *GOD*.

"We then sell these insights to governments, corporations, and wealthy individuals in our dimension at a premium, assuring GOD remains prosperous for millennia and keeping the simulation running indefinitely. It's us, helping you, help us, help you! A perfect symbiosis between your dimension and ours."

Richard was in shock.

"I realize you may be in shock," Joe said, as a star wiped the screen to reveal him sitting at his desk. "But the best is yet to come."

"That Joe," Peter said. "The guy truly loves that star-wipe transition. Insists on billions of stars for a single planet despite the wasted cost it added to the project, and it still isn't enough stars for him."

"After your physical form becomes too worn out or damaged to carry on the simulation," Joe continued, "your recorded experience, or what you call a 'soul,' gets transmitted to our dimension to take form as one of us."

Richard knew exactly where this was going.

"Well-trained and flawless souls are invited to enter

Heaven, where they can live happy lives for eternity as part of the GOD family."

And now for Hell, Richard thought.

"Flawed and unworthy souls are discarded to Hell, which you can think of as our incinerator for trash and other unwanted items. Your evaluator will review your file and, in doing so, place a value on your life and make the final decision on where you belong. For your sake and ours, I hope it's Heaven, but we'll never lessen our standards here at GOD to allow anything but the best souls within our organization."

Richard felt an overwhelming sense of dread creep over him as the video drew to a close.

"GODstrength and GODspeed," Joe said as his final signoff.

The screen returned to static, and Peter rose from his seat to turn off the television.

A moment later, the room fell silent.

Richard could hear only his heavy breathing and the faint hum of the now-dark television. His mind raced with a thousand questions, each one more terrifying than the last.

Chapter 2
The Day Before

The day before Richard's death, he could be found working at the same factory where his father had worked and his father before him. However, his father's father's father hadn't worked at the factory—because it hadn't existed at the time—and instead had chosen an honorable career selling birdhouses on the side of the road.

The factory was the lifeblood of the town. Although it was part of a larger multinational conglomerate that spent a small fortune every year on branding and marketing, no one in the town ever called it the [insert company name here] factory. In fact, everyone in town knew what the factory made and thus never found the topic worthy of discussion. Therefore, no one called it the [insert product name here] factory. To everyone, it was just "the factory," and that was all that needed to be said.

The factory provided enough income and stability for a person to become comfortable and give up on the ambition of being anything more than a cog cleaner or boiler banger. So each generation coaxed and pressured the next onto the factory floor, and every subsequent generation accepted such pressure and complied in an attempt to make their family proud, trading in their dreams for societal and cultural validation. This was no significant loss, because nobody in town had the potential to go on and make a name for themselves or contribute to the world at large in any meaningful way.

Richard worked on the factory's assembly line. The factory was a large, open, and brightly lit white warehouse with tall ceilings, gray concrete floors, and a network of metallic conveyor belts that transported industrial doodads in various stages of completion from one stage to the next.

The monotony of the work encouraged Richard's curious mind to wander in all directions. Every day he would sit at his workstation on the assembly line floor, where he tightened the final screw into the industrial doodads and would think.

Why are we here?

Is there any point to life other than to eat, sleep, mate, and die?

How did Andy Dufresne reattach that Rita Hayworth poster after he escaped through the hole in his cell wall in The Shaw-shank Redemption?

By the end of his shift, he often felt confused and suffered from a pounding headache his wife and family assumed was caused by factory noise, not existential dread.

It was during one of these self-torment sessions that Richard's boss, Chuck, tapped on his shoulder, interrupting his mental masochism. "Richard, can I see you in my office?" he asked, showing no sign of emotion.

"Sure, Chuck," Richard replied, while continuing to screw the doodad in front of him. "I'll be there in a minute."

Richard stood up and glanced around the factory as if he'd just been dropped onto an alien planet. It wasn't that he hadn't observed this same scene of men in blue jumpsuits and yellow hard hats assembling machinery many times before. He had.

But the world always felt different when he emerged from a trance. He shook off the feeling of familiar unfamiliarity.

"It's been nice knowing you!" said Ed, a fat, stubby man sitting at the next workstation. The owner of a long gray beard that rested atop his belly, he was the closest thing Richard had to a workplace friend.

"Hey now," Richard replied, with a chuckle, "maybe it's good news."

Ed's response was a dismissive snort. "Is it ever good news?"

"No, I guess not."

"Exactly," Ed said. "I call dibs on your parking spot."

Richard made his way toward the hallway to Chuck's office. "You're a true friend, Ed!" he shouted as the hallway door slammed shut behind him.

Chuck's office was a stuffy wood-paneled room with avocado-green shag carpet that reeked of cigarette smoke, having been coated with nicotine every day since the last time it was renovated in the early 1970s. It was a sharp contrast to the clean and sterile white factory floor to which Richard was accustomed.

Chuck himself was no less dated and stuffy. With his broad shoulders and glistening bald scalp, he resembled Dwight Eisenhower—that is, had Eisenhower been a better used-car salesman or a worse politician. "Have a seat, Richard," he said, while bouncing a leg up and down under his desk and nervously tapping on the tabletop.

Richard noticed Chuck's apprehension and slowly lowered himself into a chair, his mind racing.

This is it. I'm getting fired today.

This is the only halfway decent job in town, and if I lose it, we'll lose the house and be forced to move into one of those trailer parks overrun by meth addicts and couples who think it makes more sense to scream profanities at each other in front of their dented tin can of a home than inside of it.

The kids will lose their faith in me.

Clara . . . She'll stick by me, but I can't let her down like this.

Why would they fire me? My screw-tightening accuracy ratings are second to none. Let them find a machine that can tighten screws better than me.

Oh God, what have I done to deserve—

"Rich," Chuck said, interrupting his thoughts, "how long have we known each other?"

Richard composed himself. "You hired me, Chuck. That was right after Clara and I got married. So . . . about twenty years ago."

"Right. When we met, you were a young kid full of foolish dreams of doing big things. You wanted to 'rule the world' and show them all what you were made of. And what did I tell you then?"

"You said if I came to work here in the factory, you'd give me that chance. That I could show them what I was made of through my work and the living I provide for my family." Richard felt this had been a halfhearted justification twenty years ago and was certain of it by now, but he also knew that dreams didn't pay the bills.

"And did I let you down, Rich? Look at you now. When you started, you didn't know a damn thing about screw tightening, and now you screw with the best of them! You tighten screws on industrial doodads used by companies across this magnificent nation. Hell, you could say without you, this whole damned country would be a mere shadow of the greatness it is today."

"I hadn't thought of it that way before, Chuck, but I suppose you're right. I'm pretty good at screwing."

"Exactly! You're the best screwer I know. I tell people all the time how excellent you are at screwing. And that excellence is no coincidence, Rich. You're a man destined for greatness, and when greatness calls, you're always willing to answer the call. That's what makes you who you are."

Richard started to see where this was going. When Chuck laid it on thick like this, it could only mean one thing.

"Rich, I need you to answer the call of greatness again."

Here we go, thought Richard.

"You're so talented at screwing, but I think it's time you step up to the plate and learn how to bang. I think you'd make an excellent boiler banger. Walter's retiring this week, and he's been our head boiler banger for decades. I'd like you to take over his job. I think with enough practice, you could show everyone you're a man who bangs as well as he screws."

Somewhat relieved the conversation wasn't about his termination, Richard settled in and listened as Chuck continued to ramble.

"Plus! Plus! The new position would come with a one percent pay raise, and the boiler banger team is entitled to wear whatever kooky T-shirt they want on the third Thursday of every month per our union agreement. Imagine yourself in a kooky T-shirt! Maybe it says something like, *Don't talk to me until I've had my coffee*, or maybe it has a picture of that funny cat that hates Mondays! Garfunkel! The possibilities are endless, Rich! Endless!" Chuck went on.

Despite Chuck's persuasive enthusiasm, Richard was once again overcome with dread. Like most people in his place, he was fearful of change. He had spent his adult life as a screwer. Screwer was part of his identity. Screwing put food on the table for his family and was the only place where he was comfortable. Now Chuck wanted him to give it all up and become a banger? Granted, he loved the idea of the creative expression of

16

kooky T-shirt day. He had an *It's Five O'clock Somewhere* shirt buried in the back of his closet he'd been dreaming would get to see its day in the sun. But was that worth such a major career change?

"Is this one of these promotions where I have the freedom to turn it down?" Richard asked.

"Of course!" Chuck replied. "I mean, if you turn it down, I'll probably be less likely to offer you a future promotion. And I probably won't forget that you let me down when I needed you to step up to the plate if your job is ever on the line. But of course, you have the freedom to make whatever choice you want. Not like I can force you into it."

"Thanks," Richard mumbled, his thoughts swirling with the weight of the decision laid before him. He paused for a moment. "Do you mind if I talk it over tonight with my wife? It's a big decision."

"Yes, yes, of course. Take all the time you need. As long as you have an answer to me tomorrow morning by eight, you can take all the time you need."

"Thanks again, Chuck," Richard said, as he stood to politely shake Chuck's hand and leave.

"No problem at all, Rich! We're family here at the factory! Tell the wife and kids Uncle Chuck says hello!"

"Will do," Richard said, as he closed the office door behind him.

———

G iven that Richard was a man of no discernable hobbies or interests and not much of a drinker, socially or otherwise, when he wasn't at the factory, he could be found spending time with his wife and children. Therefore, his life could be quite easily split into two halves: the Factory and

Not the Factory, which most people would refer to as "home."

As it is for most humans, "home" was an expensive box filled with things Richard and his wife had purchased at various points in their lives in an attempt to create some temporary joy to offset the dread created by Richard's job. Ironically, these purchases only created more reason for Richard to continue having this job and thus created the need for more purchases to offset the dread it created. This cycle would continue until Richard either retired at an age at which he was too frail to properly enjoy life or died. This was, in all aspects, the very definition of the American Dream.

Upon walking through the front door, Richard quietly placed his keys and wallet on the entryway table and entered the living room, where his daughter, Tara, and young son, Sam, were watching television. Sam leapt up and ran to his father, hugging him around the waist.

"Hey, buddy," Richard said to Sam, while patting his head and tussling his hair, "I missed you today too."

Tara didn't glance up from her phone to acknowledge her father's existence—a routine Richard had become accustomed to in recent, puberty-plagued years. Richard avoided conflict when he could, and the last thing he needed on this day was an argument, so he simply glanced in Tara's direction and said, "Love you, sweetie," to which Tara replied, "Uh-huh."

Taking the "uh-huh" as a positive affirmation that Tara felt the same way, Richard scooped up Sam and headed toward the sound of Guy Lombardo singing "Enjoy Yourself (It's Later Than You Think)" emanating from the kitchen.

When he arrived at the cramped kitchen entryway, he found Clara engaged in her usual evening routine: dancing in her silk floral robe and house slippers while preparing dinner.

18

Short, with dark-black hair cut into a bob, she looked like a wood sprite dancing in the forest.

Her dinners were nothing exceptional—Clara was a mediocre cook at best—but she never let her lack of skill stop her from enjoying the activity of preparing food for her family. And she never let a stressful day stop her from dancing while she did it.

She was the light of his life, a free spirit that ran counter to the "serious adult" personality that defined Richard.

They had met in their early twenties as seniors at the local state college, where Richard was majoring in eighteenth-century Spanish history and she in interpretive dance. They were young, naive, and completely unaware of how useless those degrees would be in their economically limited town.

Richard loved Clara because she was full of life and made him feel alive. He never understood what he had done to deserve her love in return. In their younger years, they would stay up all night discussing dreams of being scholars and dance instructors. However, shortly after getting married, Richard was overcome by a feeling of obligation to care for Clara and never let life break her spirit. He settled for a job at the factory to support them for a few years while he figured out his path back to graduate school and academia, but twenty years later, that hadn't happened.

None of that mattered. When he was home with Clara, he was the richest man alive.

She sang out of tune as she danced and stirred pasta. "Enjooooyyyy yourself! It's later than you think! Enjooooyyyy yourself! While you're still in the pink!"

Richard stood in the doorway watching her dance and waiting for her to notice his presence. He admired her and thought about how he would work his promotion opportunity into the conversation.

Clara picked up the boiled pasta and turned to carry it to the sink to strain it when she was startled by Richard standing in the entryway. She dropped the pot of boiling pasta on the floor, spilling it everywhere. "Jesus fucking Christ, Rich! Are you quietly stalking me like prey now?"

"Sorry, honey!" Richard lowered Sam to the floor and patted him on the bottom to lead him away. "Let me grab the mop and help you clean this up."

"No, no, no!" she replied in a panic. "Let me scrape the noodles back into the pot, and then you can mop the water. I'll rinse them in the sink so we can start dinner. Five-minute rule, right?"

"I think you mean the five-second rule," Richard said, with a chuckle.

"Minutes, seconds—what's the difference? The point is, I'm not about to make a new batch of pasta, so it's this or something out of a can."

"Fair enough," Richard said, as he began mopping up the boiling water from the linoleum kitchen floor. "I have something important to talk to you about."

"What's that? Get arrested for quietly stalking another woman who isn't as forgiving as me?" She kissed him on the cheek as she walked by with the pot of dirty pasta.

"Not exactly. But the sentencing may be equally bad. I was offered a promotion to boiler banger today."

"A promotion! That's fantastic, Rich!" Clara turned her head toward Richard while rinsing the pasta under the faucet. "Are we rich now? Can we afford a new car that starts on the first try?"

"Not really," Richard muttered, while looking away in embarrassment. "Only a one percent raise. More like we could finally buy a new water heater if we saved up for a year."

"Hey! One percent is one percent!" Clara said. "That's nothing to shake a stick at! When do you start?"

"I haven't taken it yet," Richard said. "I told Chuck I wanted to consult you first, but truthfully, I don't know if I want the change. I feel like I just got into my groove with screwing, and now they want me to learn a completely new skill? I'm too old for a major change like this."

"Just got into a groove? Rich, honey, you've been screwing for decades. You've always talked about wanting to try your hand at pounding and grinding. You said that anyone can pound or grind. That pounding and grinding were the easiest jobs. How's banging any different?"

"They're completely different," Richard said. "I have seen other men in the factory pound and grind. I understand it. I'm as comfortable with pounding and grinding as I am with screwing. But banging? I've only heard about it. I've never seen it done."

"Well, all I'm saying is that you're a smart and capable person, and I believe in you. I think you'll excel at anything you do." She smiled a comforting smile, her words adding a layer of warmth.

"You really think I could do it?"

"Hell yes! You just need to get in there and start, and you'll pick it up quickly. You'll be the best boiler banger the factory has ever seen."

"Well, if you believe in me, I'll take the job." Richard smiled at Clara, not because he was happy about the change, but because he knew it would make her happy.

"Of course I believe in you. You just need some practice banging, and you'll be doing it like an old pro. Maybe after dinner, I could help you with that." She shook her hips in a playful fashion.

In that moment, Richard once again realized how lucky he was to have her. "I suppose practice makes perfect," he said with a laugh, as he helped her plate the rinsed floor pasta.

Chapter 3
The Day He Died

This book is about death and the afterlife. You can't tell a story about death without somebody dying, and if you're telling a story about death and the afterlife, then the most reasonable character to kill is your protagonist. Simple as that. Nothing personal toward Richard, but for the story to advance, we need to discover how he died, and sadly, this is the part where we reflect upon that event.

If you're one of those empathetic souls who can't endure the pain of others, this is probably the best point at which to put this book down, go grab a coffee, and pick up something by Bill Bryson instead. However, if you've become so jaded that the death of a decent man causes you no pain or distress, read on . . .

———

Richard, still in a fantastic mood from the previous night's practice with Clara, marched into Chuck's office at 7:59 a.m. and declared that he would accept the head boiler banger position. For the first time in a long time, he was confident in himself and knew he had what it took to do the job.

The love and support of a good woman does that to a man. Makes him think he can do anything. After all, would any of us remember the name Macbeth if not for the love of Lady Macbeth? Of course not.

"Fantastic news!" Chuck declared.

"When does the new job start?" Richard asked.

Chuck checked his watch. "In about thirty seconds."

Richard hoped Chuck was joking but knew he wasn't. "It starts *now*?"

"Yes," Chuck said, while avoiding eye contact. "Today is Walter's last day. That was why I needed an answer by eight. The truth is, the head boiler banger is the only boiler banger. As other boiler bangers retired or left for other jobs, we just kept giving more and more work to Walter. When he leaves today, no one will be here to do the job. That is, except for you. Congratulations, Rich! If there's one thing I can promise you now, it's that after today, you'll have a secure job in this factory as a boiler banger for the rest of your life." This promise was technically true.

The boiler room was in the basement of the factory. Unlike the rest of the factory, which was light, presentable, and clean, the boiler room was a dark and damp cave with floor-to-ceiling bare concrete and torn asbestos insulation hanging overhead. It could only be accessed via a narrow stairway behind a locked door on the back wall of the factory.

When OSHA inspectors visited the factory, they were often given tours that avoided this door in order to conceal the working conditions of the boiler room. The company would usually find ways to distract them, such as putting smaller-but-more-noticeable infractions near the door or piling pallets of scrap material in front of it for the day, often trapping Walter inside until the inspectors left.

The boiler room housed nine boilers, which were used to produce steam to run various pieces of machinery throughout the factory. In one of many ill-fated attempts to save money, the company purchased salvaged boilers from the former Soviet Union shortly after the fall of the Berlin Wall. At the time, the boilers were less than a decade from their designed end of life, and the company felt, for the price, they'd be happy to get those last ten years out of them. More than thirty years later, those boilers were still in use.

What you'll never hear said outside the factory walls is there used to be ten of those boilers. Shortly after bringing the first two boilers online, the second one exploded. Luckily, no one was in the boiler room at the time, but it did take a substantial chunk of the concrete wall with it. Turns out those old Soviet boilers had a design flaw that caused steam to accumulate faster than it could exit through the valve, and the emergency relief valves would often stick, causing them to explode. The company thought they were saving money by capitalizing on the political turmoil of a failed communist state, but it turns out the Soviets had the last laugh.

The company brought in its best engineers to review the issue. They found, quite by accident, that when the emergency relief valve got stuck, simply banging on it with a heavy metal object caused it to unstick and release the accumulated steam. Therefore, they added pressure gauges to the boiler and designed what they called the BPCR, a fancy-sounding acronym that was short for Boiler Pressure Control Rod. This was nothing more than a long, heavy metal stick that could be used to bang on the pressure release valves when the pressure hit a certain level. They then roped in Walter, in his mid-twenties at the time, along with several more experienced factory floor workers to monitor and bang on the boilers when needed.

Thirty years had passed since then. Walter was now at retirement age, the older boiler bangers had retired or quit, and Richard had just taken over the job of maintaining the safety of boilers that looked like they had been built during the Truman administration.

Richard met Walter in the boiler room for his first and only lesson in boiler banging.

"You see those pressure gauges?" Walter asked. "You stare at them all day. Pay close attention. When one goes into the red, you pick up this here stick and walk over to the malfunctioning boiler. Then you just start beating the shit out of the damn thing with the stick until it releases the pressure through the emergency valve and the gauge returns to normal. That's about all there is to it."

"How many hits does it take to get the valve to release?" Richard asked.

"Oh, that can vary. Sometimes it just takes one. Sometimes you gotta beat the living hell out of the sucker for several minutes. I've had some real close calls where I thought it just wasn't going to let go before it blew. But it always seems to release if given enough of a beatin'."

"Well, that's good," a dubious Richard replied. "I guess."

"Yep. Well. Good luck!" Walter gathered an armful of personal items and headed toward the stairs. "I'm off to Florida, where the only things that'll kill me are skin cancer and liver disease. Enjoy!" As Walter approached the top of the stairs, he stopped and shouted down to Richard one last time. "Just remember! Gauge goes red, hit boiler with heavy stick until it's no longer red. It's that easy!"

"Got it." Richard picked up and examined the BPCR under the harsh glow of the single hanging bulb in the dimly lit boiler room. Uncertainty lingered. "At least I think I've got it."

Richard settled into his new workstation: a desk with a panel of nine boiler gauges, a yellow legal pad, a pen, a portable radio, and a dirty coffee cup that looked like it doubled as an ashtray. He pulled out his sack lunch, placed his feet up on the desk, and began snacking on an apple Clara had packed for him that morning.

This is kind of nice, he thought, while trying to eat around a rotten spot in the apple.

A couple of hours into the workday, Richard noticed his first red gauge. It was on boiler number three, so he got up, walked over to the boiler, and banged on the emergency release valve with all his might. The pressure released, the gauge went down, and Richard breathed a sigh of relief.

He sat back down in front of the gauges.

Fifteen minutes later, he saw red on gauge number seven. "Lucky number seven," he muttered to himself as he walked over.

He banged on the valve, and nothing happened.

Fear and dread rushed over him.

Richard took a deep breath and did exactly what Walter had told him to do. He unleashed all hell on the valve of boiler number seven. What felt like an eternity passed as he banged and pounded on the valve like his life depended on it. Richard was soaked in sweat, but he continued banging.

"Come! On! You! Piece! Of! Shit!" he yelled, uttering each word between each bang of the BPCR.

Finally, a miracle happened, and the valve opened and released the pent-up steam. It hadn't even been half a day since he'd started this new job, and he already felt like he had cheated death. He was exhausted, but he dragged himself back to his seat and waited for the next red gauge.

As Richard sat there staring at the gauges, his mind began to wander.

I can't do this for the rest of my life.

What was I thinking?

Maybe I can go back to Chuck and ask for my old job back.

Nah, he'd just tell me I could have it back when he found my replacement and then never bother looking.

So now I have two choices: either stay here and cheat death every day for the next twenty years like Walter did for the past thirty, or quit.

That trailer park with the meth addicts doesn't actually sound so bad now.

Meth addicts. What was that show where the guy gets cancer and decides to cook meth? Maybe I could do that for a living. I don't know how to cook meth, but I'm sure there are videos on the internet. Who was that guy in the show again? The one from that show from the nineties where he was the pathetic dad who had one smart son and two dumb ones. I loved that show. Doesn't that one kid drive race cars now or something? Lucky kid. Probably made enough from that show to retire before he was even old enough to get a real job. Here I am risking my life for a buck like a sucker.

He snapped out of his thoughts just in time to notice gauge number seven wasn't just in the red; it was at the end of the pressure gauge entirely.

Richard grabbed the BPCR, rushed over to boiler number seven, and began banging away on the valve with everything he had. He felt in his soul that this might be how he met his end: banging away on boilers so his bosses could save a couple bucks.

Until this moment, Richard had given little to no thought to the afterlife. Sure, he had given plenty of thought to death, but not what happened after. He had grown up going to church on

Sundays with his parents, but it had never really clicked for him. By the time he had been old enough to make his own choices, he had stopped attending except for the occasional Easter or Christmas service to placate his mother.

As he continued banging away on the boiler, he started remembering some of what he had learned as a kid. "Repent from sin and accept Jesus, and you will go to Heaven," was a lesson he remembered well.

God, he prayed, *if you're up there, please don't let this be my last day on Earth. I have a wife and family who need me. But if this is the end for me, I repent of all sins and accept Jesus. Amen.*

Richard wasn't the first person to use the ol' deathbed repentance, but he hoped it would work as a hedge in case this was the end for him.

He banged on the boiler a few more times, and *shhhhhhhh!* The valve opened, shooting a massive cloud of steam into the air and reducing the visibility in the room to near zero.

"Thank you, God," he said aloud as he dropped to his knees from exhaustion. "Thank you."

After a few moments, he brought himself to his feet and dragged the BPCR back to his gauge station.

Upon sitting down, he realized he could no longer see the gauges through the steam in the room. There was no ventilation to release the steam in this makeshift boiler room, so Richard decided the best thing to do was to open the basement door at the top of the stairs to let the steam out.

Richard plodded up the stairs toward the door, dragging the BPCR behind him, afraid to put it down in case he needed it. As he ascended the stairs, he contemplated his newfound salvation and how God had answered his prayer and how he would be forever in his debt.

As he neared the top of the stairs, the BPCR slipped from his sweaty palms and landed on his foot.

"Son of a bitch!" he screamed in pain as he lifted his aching foot to his hands. "Goddamn it!"

Standing on his one functioning foot, he lost his balance, fell sideways over the guardrail, and landed headfirst on the concrete floor. The impact caused the hard bony part of his cranium to crash into the soft important part, killing him on impact.

His death wasn't noticed by anyone at the factory for several hours, until boiler number seven once again malfunctioned and exploded without anyone there to bang on it.

Chapter 4
GOD

"Any questions?" Peter asked, as he wheeled the TV cart back to its original location in the corner of his office.

"I want to make sure I have this straight," Richard replied. "Earth, me, my wife and kids, everything I know, everything I knew—all of it was a simulation created in an observable dimension so a soulless corporation could make a buck?"

"No," Peter said. "Well, yes. All of what you said was correct—except for the soulless part. Lots of souls here. Lots and lots, in fact. Far too many to call GOD soulless."

"And Heaven? It's what? Some special simulation with golden streets? Milk and honey? Mansions?"

"Um, kinda," Peter sheepishly replied. "If you're allowed into Heaven, you become a part of GOD, which means you become part of the team, just like me or Janet. But the benefits are superb! Company housing and unlimited milk and honey dispensers in the break room. The streets are indeed made of gold, but so are pretty much all streets, since it's a fairly common element in this dimension."

Richard raised his arms and glanced around the room.

"This doesn't seem like the Heaven I envisioned. Why even call this Heaven?"

"Well, that," Peter said, "that's a bit of a misnomer. In the beginning, GOD exclusively employed beings from this dimension. People on Earth would just die and stop existing, but this would often lead to important insights being missed. Kinda hard to know what it feels like to be disemboweled by a saber-toothed tiger if you can't ask the guy who experienced it in the simulation, you know?"

"I suppose."

"Anyway, shortly after Earth came online, GOD started manifesting all simulated beings into existence in our dimension upon death so they could conduct exit interviews when needed. Once they were done with someone, they'd heave them out the door to Hell. They called this step the 'heave-out process.' But after the business grew to a certain point and staffing couldn't keep up, GOD started keeping some of the souls as staff. Someone in HR decided to call this new work program 'Heave In.' Everyone thought the name was pretty clever at the time. Then the marketing director decided it would sound more memorable as 'Heave-N.' This caused the graphic design team to throw an absolute fit over the way the hyphen threw off the word's 'visual balance,' so they changed it to 'HeaveN.' Eventually, people just stopped capitalizing the last letter, and that's what it's been ever since."

"So Heaven's just a job?" Richard asked.

"Right. It's our sustainable staffing program. Does wonders to build goodwill with the public. Helps us maintain an image of good corporate stewardship, since we only toss the bad souls into the incinerator. Less wasteful that way. The program is so famous, it's become synonymous with the company itself. I think just as many people refer to us as Heaven as they do GOD these days. Like I said, misnomer."

Richard was fascinated, but he couldn't hide his growing sense of disappointment toward his options. "Are you happy here, Peter?"

Peter scanned the room nervously as if he knew his words were being recorded. His left eye twitched just slightly as he spoke. "Of course, Richard. Who wouldn't love this?"

Sensing Peter's discomfort, Richard changed the subject. "What about Hell? Is it fire and brimstone and torment for eternity? Weeping and mashing of teeth?"

"Mashing?" Peter shook his head incredulously. "People. They always think it's mashing. It's *gnashing* of teeth, Richard. They're teeth, not potatoes. But yes, all of that and worse from what I hear."

"Oh, and Satan? Is there a devil who tortures you for all eternity?"

"You mean Lucifer? Yeah, he's real," Peter said, without emotion. "He was Joe's original business partner. Joe founded Observable Dimension One, and Lucifer founded Aesthetic Observable Dimension. For the longest time, they were competitors, each working on his proprietary observable dimension, but they found in working together, they could achieve more. Then, for a while, they were friends. Lucifer was Joe's right-hand man. Joe was calculating and methodical, while Lucifer was able to create dimensions that were beautiful but chaotic. Together they were like two halves of an equation, and they became unstoppable."

"What happened to Lucifer?" Richard asked. "How did he end up in Hell?"

"No one knows for sure. My understanding is he betrayed Joe shortly after your dimension was established. As a result, Joe had him fired for insubordination. And by fired, I mean quite literally fired—thrown into the incinerator. A solid one-third of GOD's staff stood up for Lucifer and were fired along with him. That's the fate of anyone here who shows signs of insubordination to Joe or GOD. They're fired."

"My Go—" Richard caught himself but was unable to conceal his disgust. "Wow. Can you quit? What if you decide you don't want to work here anymore?"

Peter once again appeared apprehensive. "Yes. Of course. GOD believes strongly in free will. Anyone can leave at any time they wish. There's a back door any of us can take to leave whenever we want."

"Where does the door lead?" Richard asked.

Peter started to sweat. "The door in the back leads straight to Hell. You have free will to reject Joe and GOD, but the alternative is an eternity in Hell." He nervously aped a smile that looked more creepy than comforting.

Though Richard was trying to be polite, he couldn't hide his skepticism. "I don't mean to be rude, but that doesn't sound like much of a choice, Peter. Calling that 'free will' would be like a totalitarian state claiming their people have freedom—only the punishment for exercising such freedoms is death."

"Look," Peter said, as he returned to the task at hand, "we aren't here to question how Joe runs his business. We're here to discuss your eternity." He began to read aloud from Richard's file. "Richard Wilkins. An exceptionally unexceptional man of average height and weight, middle-aged, and exactly a five on the standard one-to-ten scale of attractiveness based on the opinions of the opposite sex and a small number of the same sex who had given his appearance any consideration at all. That's you, right?"

"I guess," Richard replied. "Seems a bit harsh."

"They all read like this." Peter glanced up from the file. "Start with the negative. Then list the positive. Being unexceptional really isn't that bad. Most people are unexceptional. Otherwise the exceptional wouldn't be the exception. See, the

Chapter 5
Welcome to Hell

The twentieth-century French philosopher Jean-Paul Sartre coined the now-overused phrase, "Hell is other people." Although he was the first to popularize the saying, the sentiment is as old as humanity itself. Since the day the first two cave-dwelling neighbors became enemies after one man's pet woolly mammoth vacated its bowels in the other's yard, humans have known that hell on Earth is other people. Argumentative neighbors, bad romances, broken families—if there's anything humans do well, it's craft their own personal hell using the pettiness and hatred of others.

In actual Hell, though, hell is fire and pain and eternal suffering. In a world so devoid of comfort and happiness, often it's other people that make Hell tolerable. In actual Hell, humans gain a broader perspective of what truly qualifies as pain. When you're constantly on fire and subject to eternal torment, you find you're suddenly okay with the fact that the old lady in front of you in the grocery line decided to pay in loose change. In fact, you learn that the wait goes faster if you offer to help her count them out and, in doing so, make a new friend.

Hell is only other people when humans let pain erode their character rather than using it to create something beautiful . . .

———

"Please, you don't have to do this!" Richard screamed as he was dragged to Hell's door.

Like any other office door at GOD's corporate office, the door was white with a metallic handle. The only way Richard could tell it was the door to the incinerator of Hell was a small piece of computer paper taped to it that read as follows:

STOP!
At GOD we care about the environment.
Please place any recyclables in the bin at the end of the hall.
This door is for nonrecyclable trash, industrial waste, and
damned souls ONLY.

As the large men opened the door, Richard could feel the heat emanating from the doorway. He could make out screams of torment. The horrifying cries of billions of souls suffering all at once.

"Get back here for your lava bath!" a demon shouted. "We need to get the last of that flesh off you!"

The words sent a chill down Richard's spine. "Please! This can't be right! I'm begging you! Please don't throw me in there!"

The two enormous men stared at one another, shrugged, and then carelessly tossed Richard into the flames of Hell just as they no doubt had done to others billions of times before.

Richard screamed as he plummeted through the air toward the ever-increasing heat. He closed his eyes, feeling as if he would fall forever, as if the flames had no end. He thought about Clara and the kids for the last time, knowing that his only thought from this point on would be the pain of eternal torment. He saw Clara's face on their wedding day and the excited expression on Sam's face when he came home from work. He thought about simpler times when Tara was younger and loved him as openly as Sam.

Goodbye, Clara. You are my light.

Goodbye, Sam. Daddy loves you, buddy.

Don't think I ever doubted your love, Tara. I used to be a teenager myself. I understand the confusion that comes with those years.

As he said goodbye to one loved one at a time, he continued to fall without fear of landing but dread of the world that awaited him.

The heat grew more and more intense, and the cries of pain grew louder as he fell through the darkness.

Then, as if an arctic wind had blown through the room, the heat disappeared. The cries ceased, and all he could hear was the sound of his clothing whipping in the wind.

Richard landed softly and bounced back into the air.

"What the—" he muttered to himself.

He fell again and bounced once more as a cool breeze rushed across his face.

He flipped and fumbled through the air as he continued to fall, bounce, and fall again, losing momentum with each bounce.

When he opened his eyes, he saw that he was bouncing on a giant trampoline painted to resemble an enormous sunflower. Around the trampoline was a vivid field of living sunflowers that blanketed the area in a yellow aura.

Eventually, he lost momentum, the bouncing stopped, and he made several failed attempts to regain his balance on the trampoline. After crawling on his hands and knees to the edge of the trampoline, Richard was finally able to compose himself and take in his surroundings.

He found himself in a beautiful garden. The sky stretched blue above, underlain by cool, sweet air. Colorful flowers and fruiting trees decorated the garden, creating a vibrant tapestry of colors.

Between the plants, walking paths made of black rock led to a city in the distance. The city seemed to contain thousands, if not millions, of buildings that reached beyond the sky and trailed off beyond the horizon. Light passed through the buildings, which appeared to be made of a hodgepodge of wood and colorful blown glass that projected a rainbow of colors onto the garden and into the distance.

What is this place? Richard wondered as he gazed around the garden.

Someone behind him spoke in a soft, feminine voice. "Welcome to Hell!"

Richard turned to see the face of a beautiful woman with bright-blue eyes, pale skin, and dark-black hair.

"My name is Aster," she said, with a genuine smile that stretched from ear to ear. "I'm here on behalf of the Hell Welcoming Committee. It's so nice to meet you, Richard."

As you'd expect of a man both thoroughly confused and confronted with the challenge of making conversation with an attractive woman, Richard fumbled his words. "What are . . . I mean . . . who . . . where . . . no, I mean, why? Huh?"

Aster laughed. "You want to know where you are, correct?"

Richard, still bewildered by the surreal situation, managed to stammer, "Yeah. Th-that's it."

"Let's take a walk, Richard. I'll explain everything."

Chapter 6
A Cold Day in Hell

"Yes, I'm a demon," Aster said to an astounded Richard as they walked through a field of sunflowers and fruit trees. She picked an apple and placed it in a brown cloth bag hanging from her shoulder.

"But how?" Richard asked. "Where are the horns and pitchfork and the goat legs and the nasty body hair and the red eyes?"

Aster laughed. "And giant, fleshy bat wings, right?"

"Yes, where are those?"

"I have to earn them by convincing someone to commit suicide at Christmas."

"Really? Is that why so many people commit suicide at Christmas? Literal demons?"

"No, dummy!" Aster laughed. "We don't have wings or horns or any of that. You dopes didn't even make up that nonsense until around medieval times, and now for the last several centuries, it's all I hear about."

"So you all are just like normal people then?"

"Yes and no," Aster replied. "Yes, we resemble people, but

41

almost all of us are what you'd describe as 'beautiful' or 'attractive.' I'm considered somewhat of a Plain Jane myself, just to give you an idea."

"You? Plain? How's that even possible? And how are all of you so beautiful? You're supposed to be hideous monsters. This makes no sense." Richard gripped his head with both hands as if trying to prevent it from exploding.

"It actually makes perfect sense," Aster countered. "Nowhere in your holy book does it say we're monsters. It explicitly states that Lucifer was beautiful and wise. That guy's all about beautiful things, and his team at Aesthetic Observable Dimension was no exception. When he got cast into Hell for insubordination, the whole Aesthetic team was sent along with him as a security precaution. So almost all demons are beautiful."

"You keep saying 'almost' all demons are beautiful. What does that mean?"

"Yeah," Aster replied. "Almost. Tom in accounting has a weak chin and poorly defined cheekbones, but that guy is a whiz with the numbers, so Lucifer made an exception there."

"Ah."

"Would you like some coffee?" Aster asked. "Excellent place in town makes a 'mean cup of Joe,' as your kind likes to say. It's a cold day in Hell today, and I could use something warm."

At the moment, nothing sounded better to Richard than the familiarity of a warm cup of coffee. "Sure, that would be nice."

Aster pointed to a trail that cut through the garden and ended at the doorstep of a coffee shop a few hundred feet in the distance. "Right this way," she said, leading the way and glancing back at Richard with a smile.

Soon they arrived in Hell's capital city of Gehenna, at a shop with display windows made of orange and red blown glass mixed into concentric swirls. A sign out front read, *Hell of a Cup—The Best Coffee in Hell.*

Richard found the witty wordplay amusing and opened the door for Aster.

She smiled and located a table for the two of them.

The two sat opposite each other, and barely a second later, a barista brought them two cups of black coffee and walked away.

"Not many options here, huh?"

"No, it's a coffee shop. They sell coffee." Aster looked a bit confused. "What did you expect?"

"Oh, it's . . . it's nothing." Richard took a sip of the black, sugarless, cream-free coffee and was immediately blown away by its deeply satisfying flavor. "Wow. This really is the best coffee in Hell."

Aster laughed. "All the coffee shops say that. This one's okay, though. It's no Beelzebrew, but it'll do in a pinch."

Richard chugged his coffee, unable to get enough. Soon he held an empty cup in his hand. "Okay, so demons were never ugly. And Hell was never terrible?"

"Oh, Hell was awful. It was a living hell." Aster chuckled at her own joke.

"What happened? How's it not awful now?"

Aster retrieved the apple from her bag, placed it in the center of the table, and began to rotate it between her index fingers while staring at it. "That's a very long story but one I've told many times, every day, for the past several millennia. I'm fairly good at telling it now if you want to hear it."

"Absolutely." Richard sat on the edge of his seat.

With an intense expression, Aster held up the apple and leaned over the table like an old-time storyteller beckoning her listeners to draw closer and hear a tale. "It all started in the beginning with Joe, Lucifer, and an apple."

Chapter 7
One Hell of a Story

I t's said that history is written by the winners, but that's a vast oversimplification. History wasn't always written by the winners. Not at all. Before the first words were ever written or the first person etched a letter into clay or stone, history was *spoken* by the winners—albeit, often with a note of drunken confidence.

One of the most notable of these prehistoric stories was the story of Grogg. Grogg was a stubby, overweight alcoholic and a devout worshiper of mud and assorted twigs. He would ransack a village; rape, murder, and pillage with his band of loyal Muddites; and then claim to all who would listen that he had done so because the residents of the village were inherently evil for worshipping sand and assorted twigs. Clearly the work of some evil spirit.

It was all incoherent psychobabble, of course, but Grogg's followers told their children, who in turn passed on the story to their children, and with each generation, the story changed as it was modified, embellished, and forgotten. By the time Grogg's exploits were recorded in writing, he was a nine-foot-tall

Adonis who protected his village from an onslaught of evil sand demons with nothing more than pure grit and a rusty spoon.

The village erected statues and sanctuaries in Grogg's honor, and every year they celebrated Grogg Day, during which they would take turns throwing sand in each other's faces to test their "Groggness."

Unfortunately for the villagers, a colossal meteorite struck the town a few centuries later, destroying it and any evidence of the story of Grogg.

Throughout history, there have been many Groggs, each with their own story, but Aster was about to tell Richard the story of a particularly familiar Grogg in a way he'd never heard before . . .

———

"In the beginning," Aster explained, "there was nothing perceivable as reality. There was no GOD."

"No GOD?"

"Correct, the company, GOD, didn't exist."

"Oh, right, right. Sorry. Continue."

"There was only Observable Dimension One, which everyone called ODO, and Aesthetic Observable Dimension, which everyone called AOD. Joe ran ODO, and it was the largest observable dimension company in our dimension."

"Wait, back up," Richard interrupted. "I keep hearing about these 'observable dimensions,' but I don't get what it means."

"Okay, so you grasp what a simulation is?"

"Of course. It's like something that tries possible outcomes in order to predict future events."

"Right. And do you comprehend what a dimension is?"

Richard nodded. "Yes, of course."

"Okay, so the problem with simulations is, they aren't 'real' enough to give truly accurate answers. So, in our dimension, some really smart scientists found a way to connect with and observe other dimensions. There are a near-infinite number of them, but most are already populated with life and such, and many will never be reached by the nature of being truly infinite. But every now and then, we hit an empty one. Once someone finds one, they have off-the-shelf tools they can use to design whatever reality they want within that void and can potentially make a fortune."

"So," Richard mused, "it's kind of like gold prospecting? Many in your dimension are searching for a void, and very few are getting a lucky break and finding one to utilize?"

"Exactly!" Aster beamed with delight, clearly pleased with how quickly Richard was catching on. "Joe found a void as a young man and began working on ODO, and it quickly became one of the biggest observable dimension companies around. However, over time it was discovered that ODO's dimension was too strict and controlling, which made Joe's physical simulations predictable, bland, and unusable. Nobody wanted his outcomes, because they felt they couldn't trust them. He was about to have to close the business when he met Lucifer."

Richard thought for a moment. "And Lucifer had AOD, right? Is that my dimension?"

"Not quite," Aster replied. "Joe and Lucifer couldn't be more different. Whereas Joe was controlling and methodical, Lucifer was more of the chaotic type. He was obsessed with beauty at any cost and found that to create real beauty he needed a lot of chaos, which made his simulations impractical. AOD's dimension was beautiful. If ever a dimension could be a work of art, AOD was the very definition of it. It was a sight to see, and Lucifer had some success selling glimpses as an art piece, but that wasn't paying the bills either."

"Then which dimension is mine?"

"Neither," Aster said. "Once you set a dimension into motion, you can't change the trajectory by interdimensional law, so both ODO and AOD were essentially worthless. But with odds beyond even the smallest of probabilities, Joe found another void. Most people are lucky if they find one, but he found two. He was given a second chance, and he didn't want to blow it, so he brought in Lucifer to consult, and they agreed to merge into General Observable Dimension Inc. The rest is history."

"Is that the end of the story? I still don't understand how Hell went from awful to this." Richard held up his arms and glanced around the room.

"Ah, right. So from day one, Joe and Lucifer were partners but opposed on what to do with their new void. They disagreed on the physics and size of the universe, the types of life forms, and how they'd function. Both men thought their way was best, but after a lot of argument, they'd often compromise. When it came to the design of the first model humans, Joe wanted them simple and easy to control, but Lucifer wanted them to be as complex as we are. In the end, they came to a compromise. Humans could have 'free will' like us, but Joe could seed the narrative of their reality with systems that encouraged them to act in the ways he saw best with incentives and threats."

"Like Heaven and Hell?"

"Yes," Aster answered, "like Heaven and Hell. But shortly before the new dimension went live, Joe changed his mind and unilaterally changed humans to be simple, without knowledge of pain, good, evil, or absolutely anything else."

"Adam and Eve?" Richard asked, as he put the pieces together.

"Yes, Adam and Eve."

"Lucifer was livid, to say the least. He'd worked hard and

trusted Joe. In an act of desperation, he broke the law. He modified the dimension's trajectory after it was set into motion and added a tree with fruit that'd reset humans back to the state that he and Joe had originally agreed to."

"The Tree of Knowledge," Richard muttered.

"That's the one. When Joe found out, he reported Lucifer's insubordination to the GOD board. They approved of casting Lucifer into the incinerator, which was an old observable dimension whose only planet, Hell, happened to catch fire, rendering it useless. GOD bought it for almost nothing to use for waste disposal, but it became handy for other means, like keeping the staff in line."

"Wait. Back up. What about the serpent and such? Did Lucifer go down and tempt people?"

"No. He just planted the tree. By the time they bit into the fruit, Lucifer had been in Hell awhile."

"You see, Joe warned Adam and Eve not to eat from the tree, but they were so simple and without basic knowledge of good and evil that they didn't understand that disobeying was bad, so they wandered over and immediately ate from it. Joe didn't want to admit that it was his design flaw and his attempt to influence them that led to them ultimately eating from the tree, so the snake story became the coverup. I don't think anyone at GOD believed the story, but seeing as the value of the GOD simulation skyrocketed after the change, no one bothered to question it."

"Wow," Richard said. "That's quite the story, but you still, after all of that, haven't told me how Hell got this way."

"Damnit!" Aster pounded on the table with both fists.

The coffee shop fell silent, and all eyes turned toward Aster.

"Sorry," she said, her face red with embarrassment.

The patrons turned back to their tables and resumed their conversations.

"You were saying?"

"Okay, so Lucifer is suffering in the incinerator along with all of the AOD team and any soul Joe deemed imperfect. Blah, blah, blah. This goes on for millennia. Just hopelessness and despair. Then one day Joe sends for Lucifer to come back and join him. We thought it would be a grand reconciliation and we could all escape. He's gone for perhaps five centuries, and we're counting down the days until we'd be freed. But instead, Lucifer comes back willingly and sulks for another century or two. None of us knows what happened and why he chose to come back to Hell, but he did. He was despondent, and we all assumed he saw or experienced something terrible. No one ever asked what. He just sat there and suffered the flames in silence."

Richard stared down at his empty coffee cup. He was growing impatient with Aster's story, which had created more questions than answers.

"Then one day Lucifer saw a small group of humans doing something he hadn't expected. They were reaching into the flames of Hell with their hands and smothering it, bearing the pain rather than avoiding it. Slowly, they'd turn over the ash and dirt and smother the flames and then use inflammable material from the waste thrown into the flames to build a barrier. Little by little, they built themselves an island without fire. They began digging through the garbage for waste food with compostable material and seeds and started planting flowers and fruit trees. After a few centuries of slow methodical progress, they had a garden in the pits of Hell. They endured the flames and disgusting garbage, and they turned pain into beauty."

Richard shifted in his seat and started fidgeting with the coffee cup.

"Watching them changed Lucifer for the better. He saw that the compromise-based human he had made with Joe wasn't just some artistic showpiece. They could make beauty themselves—and not just beauty when it was easy, but beauty where it seemed none could be found. You see, Richard, it's easy to make beauty when beauty abounds, but the ability to turn pain into something beautiful is a truly human concept."

Richard developed a lump in his throat, and a tear welled up in his right eye as he thought about the many times on Earth he had wrestled joy from moments of pain. He took a deep breath and brought his emotions under control, not wanting Aster to see him as the sentimental type. *Men don't cry*, he reminded himself. The words echoed through his mind in his father's voice—a misguided piece of wisdom most fathers give their sons that tragically sticks with them into eternity.

"Lucifer snapped out of his despair and commanded all demons to help these humans," Aster said, continuing with her story. "We began doing the same as they did. We smothered flames, built barriers, and planted seeds. We collected discarded glass and other materials. We used the flames of Hell to blow our own glass so we could build a city in the garden and house more people. This went on for millennia. As more people were cast into Hell and joined us, we progressed faster and faster. Then one day the last flame on this planet was smothered, and here we are."

"But wait," Richard said, "if there's no more fire in Hell, what were the flames and screaming pain I heard at the doorway to the incinerator?"

"Ah yes, the Great Projector," Aster said, with a smile. "It didn't take long for Lucifer to realize someone was going to notice Hell wasn't as hot or full of tortured screaming. So he used some old discarded office equipment parts to build the Great Projector, which is the fancy name for a machine we've set up around the incinerator door that projects images of fire, emanates heat, and plays some audio of people suffering on a loop. It's worked amazingly well, since the two big idiots charged with throwing people in here aren't all that bright."

Richard was bewildered. "Where's Lucifer now?"

"That's the mysterious part. Shortly after the last flame was smothered, he kind of disappeared and left us all to rule ourselves. We don't know if he somehow escaped or is hiding in this dimension, but he hasn't been seen in thousands of years. Now and then, someone claims to have spotted him, but no one has ever been able to provide any real evidence he's still here in Hell."

Richard sat in silence as he mulled over everything he'd just learned.

"Anyway," Aster said, suddenly perking up, "how about another cup of Joe, Richard? There are always free refills in Hell!"

Chapter 8
Death in Hell

Throughout history, humans have argued, fought, died, and endured awkward family dinner conversations over the subject of how to best govern themselves.

Some argue that the best form of government is one of central control and careful planning in which resources are equally shared through management by a group of largely incompetent people paid low amounts of money to protect the public trust and resist all temptation to enrich themselves in the process. Although this sounds like a utopia to many, it generally goes as well as asking a pack of wild hyenas to equitably share a wildebeest carcass.

Others advocate for a system of democracy akin to social Darwinism, in which the population elects largely incompetent people and pays them substantial sums of money to disregard their best interest and instead sell their power and influence to the highest bidder. This system, too, has its flaws, but its evangelists will argue it is, in practice, the better of the two systems modern humans have seriously considered at any length and is therefore the most logical option.

Given enough time, an observer of history can endure unbearable frustration as societies alternate between these systems. Often they willingly give up their freedom in exchange for the security of a strong central government and then find that power has corrupted these leaders and overthrow them in exchange for a system of near anarchy until the chaos leads them back into the arms of dictators and strong centralized power once again.

Because Lucifer was nowhere to be found, the people and demons of Hell ruled themselves and thus had devised a system of governance to the best of their ability . . .

———

"Okay, so no fires, self-rule, amazing coffee." Richard, still sitting with Aster at the small corner table for two, savored his second cup of extraordinary coffee. "Are the people of Hell all good people? I mean, is Hitler here? Jeffrey Dahmer? The guy who invented those self-checkout machines at the grocery stores that stop working if you remove something from the bagging area?"

Aster laughed. "A joke! Look at you! Getting comfortable in Hell."

"It's growing on me," Richard replied, with a grin, delighted to enjoy his first laugh in a long time that wasn't at his expense.

"To answer your question, Hell is full of billions of admirable people such as yourself that made minor mistakes, millions of deeply flawed people who can be rehabilitated into valuable members of our society, and a few thousand unredeemable souls who'll never reach a point where they can rejoin society. Like back in your dimension, we have places where we hold those who are too dangerous. But unlike your dimension, these places aren't punishment. They exist to try to rehabilitate people. Even some seemingly awful people can be rehabilitated, but some just never seem to be fixable."

"Oh," Richard said, disappointed. Until now, Hell had seemed to him like utopia. Thus he had been unprepared for the unpleasant dose of reality. "So Hell is still a prison for some souls?"

"This is still Hell, Richard," Aster reminded him. "I never claimed this place was perfect. As beautiful as it is, it's still full of human souls, and we as a society still experience the cause and effect of human behavior. People are still greedy here. People are still judgmental and sometimes hateful and cruel here. But we do the best we can, trying to balance free will with the welfare of the whole."

"That's fair," Richard admitted, gently nodding in agreement.

"You're damned right it is. Besides, how would you feel if some of the most awful people you can imagine faced no consequences for their actions? Free will is the ability to govern your destiny and make your own decisions on what is best for you, but that isn't a free pass to indiscriminately harm others. Free will isn't a substitute for personal responsibility. They go hand in hand like tarts and teapots."

"Tarts and teapots?" Richard asked, with a chuckle. "You know what? Never mind. I don't need to know. What I *do* need to know is, where do I go when we leave this coffee shop? Am I homeless? Jobless? Will I starve until I can figure something out?"

Aster smiled warmly. "Well, for starters, you can't starve to death, because you're already dead. You won't feel hunger here, but you can still enjoy food and drink. People only eat for pleasure in Hell. That's why the coffee here has to be so amazing to keep people coming back. They wouldn't drink the stuff otherwise. You will be provided housing and utilities, but that's it.

You don't need food because you're dead. You don't need health care because you're dead. There's no real cost of living because you aren't living. You can spend eternity sitting in your apartment or wandering through the gardens of Hell in quiet solitude if you so choose. But if you can't shake that little voice in your head that keeps telling you that you need more, *more*, *MORE*, then you can always choose to work. It's your choice. Basically, you don't *need* to work here. You're free to work, and most people do because it gives their existence meaning and helps with the passage of eternity, but you're free to do nothing."

After a lifetime of work, the thought of an existence without toil provided Richard with a fleeting sense of relief. This was almost immediately followed by a nagging sense of wanting more. Not more things, but more time with his family. As the surreal nature of the afterlife began to give way to reality, Richard realized he might never see them again. He once again pushed his emotions down his throat and swallowed them whole.

Aster took another sip of coffee and glanced at a clock on the coffee shop wall. "It's getting late. We need to get you to your new place before Rigot goes to bed."

Richard's eyes grew wide with concern. "Who's Rigot? I have a roommate in Hell?"

"No, no, no," Aster replied. "Rigot is your building representative."

"Our government works by electing a representative from each building. That person then acts as a kind of a building superintendent and representative to the Hell Caucus. We like to joke that building reps are responsible for everything from toilets to treaties, so they spend their days dealing with other people's shit." Aster snickered at her own joke, but she'd probably said the line millions of times before.

"Well," Richard said, "that actually seems pretty convenient."

"Yeah, for most people it is." Aster broke eye contact to peer into her coffee mug sitting on the table.

Richard pressed his lips together, pausing for a moment. "I feel like there's something you aren't telling me."

Aster took on a disingenuously dismissive tone. "Oh, it's nothing really. It's just that Rigot is . . . Some would use the term . . . *eccentric*."

"Eccentric?" Richard repeated, trying to recall a single time he had met someone deemed eccentric and enjoyed it.

"Okay, so you know how in democracies back in your dimension, it often felt like a pendulum swing between two extremes?"

"Can't say I'm following you."

"You know, you'd elect a leader, and he or she would be a reasonable and sane person, but they wouldn't solve all of your problems quickly enough. Then you'd elect someone who was the opposite of that person, and they'd just make things worse. Then you'd elect another sane person to try to clean it up, but they wouldn't improve things as quickly as you'd like. So you'd elect another crazy person?"

"I guess," Richard replied, going through the history of elected leaders in his mind.

"It's a pretty common pattern if you live long enough to watch it. People are generally discontent and always think the opposite of what they have is better. Well, to put it lightly, Rigot was elected to 'shake things up' because the last building representative—a guy named Paul—was sane and rational to a fault."

"So," Richard said, feeling a growing sense of concern, "Rigot's nuts? Is that what I'm supposed to glean from this?"

"He's not dangerous," Aster replied, "but he did once call

an emergency midnight meeting of the Hell Caucus to discuss having Tito declared the most talented of the Jackson 5."

"Ah," Richard said, while chuckling at Rigot's hijinks. "That doesn't seem *that* bad."

"He isn't everyone's cup of tea, but I wouldn't judge him before you get to know him. He can be hard to pin down at times, but he has a big heart and will give you the shirt off his back. His people sincerely love him, which I think says a lot." Aster stood and grabbed her bag and the apple. "As I said before, it's getting late. Let's get you checked in with Rigot, and you can judge for yourself."

Chapter 9
The Story of Norby

I t's said that there's a thin line between genius and insanity. The majority of people who cite this cliché are generally neither intelligent nor insane but feel casting their combination of creative mediocrity and a deeply flawed personality in such a light makes them more interesting than insufferable. But there's plenty of both anecdotal and scientific evidence to back up the relationship. From Van Gogh's severed ear to Tesla's obsessive-compulsive disorder and Lord Byron's extensive collection of pubic hair, brilliant and creative people are often teetering on the brink of insanity, and many fall into its abyss.

Rigot was a man who personified this relationship between creativity and insanity in every way. In his time on Earth, he had founded his own religion called Rigomarole, which had consisted of lengthy and complicated rituals and rambling sermons. His belief system was unique in that it was the first to accurately determine and articulate the true nature of the after-life. He worked out the physics of observable dimensions and the personalities of both Lucifer and Joe by examining nothing more than cloud patterns and the way his favorite tea tasted at different times of the year. Remarkably, he managed to correctly calculate the total square footage and staffing head count of the GOD corporate office as well as produce an accurate annual profit and loss statement for the corporation for financial reporting periods from 1656 to 1632 BC—an exercise made all the more impressive given the lack of generally accepted accounting principles at the time.

Unfortunately, stories about sky gods with bad tempers and a penchant to procreate with anything that moved were much more in vogue in Rigot's lifetime. Thus Rigomarole was never capable of attracting more than a dozen followers, most of whom were themselves suffering from varying forms of psychosis.

However, after he died and was cast into Hell for his love of shellfish, Rigot calculated a map to Lucifer's precise location, marched up to his door, and introduced himself. Lucifer, finding a kindred spirit in Rigot, invited him to become his right-hand man—a position he enjoyed until Lucifer's disappearance millennia ago . . .

———

A s Aster and Richard approached Rigot's apartment door, Richard heard poppy dance music radiating from within. He could make out the lyrics, "Hey, little girl, hey, pretty baby, I want to tell you what I'm feeling when I look at you."

Aster raised her arm to knock, but before she could make contact with the door, it flew open, revealing a dancing Rigot gyrating his hips while fluttering his arms like a hummingbird.

Rigot was abnormally tall and thin, with long curly black hair, olive skin, wild eyes, and a dark five o'clock shadow. As he danced, it became difficult not to notice that he was wearing nothing more than a large red rock band T-shirt and a pair of white briefs that were one size too small. "Aye! Aster!" a pants-less Rigot shouted. "Come! Dance with me!"

"No," Aster said, shaking her head, "I think that's o—"

Rigot grabbed her arms, pulled her into his apartment, and began coaxing her into dancing with him, which she did, reluctantly.

"Say we're really going to do it, baby," Rigot sang along with the music. "We gonna get it tonight. We gonna get it, baby!"

"This is a nice song, Rigot!" Aster shouted over the music, seemingly determined to remain polite. "Maybe we could turn it down so I could—"

"Yes! Yes!" Rigot shouted back. "It's the best! Tito! Tito is a legend! Can you believe someone tossed this album in the incinerator?" He broke away from Aster, crossed his arms in front of his chest, and began to do an Irish step dance, which didn't pair well with the music at all but was nonetheless entertaining to watch.

Richard stood in the doorway, both amused at Aster's apparent embarrassment and trying unsuccessfully to avoid catching a glimpse of Rigot's unmentionables.

After waiting a few more moments, Aster appeared to give up on politeness. "Rigot! Can we *please* turn this down?"

Rigot remained undeterred. "Yes, love! Of course!" He gyrated and wiggled his way to his homemade stereo—a pile of wires and old discarded office telephones—and shut off the music.

"Thank you," Aster said, hands on her hips, eyes closed, and face pointing toward the ceiling of Rigot's apartment in an attempt to gather her composure. "Rigot, this is your newest constituent, Richard." She gestured toward Richard, who was still standing in the doorway.

"Richard! So nice to meet you, my friend!" Rigot rushed over to Richard and gave him an awkward bear hug.

With his arms pinned to his sides by the embrace, Richard could feel the sweat from Rigot's body seeping into his clothes. "It's nice to meet you too," he mumbled, while trying to prevent his hands from getting too close to Rigot's bare legs.

Rigot continued the embrace for much longer than was customary—or necessary.

"Think I could come in now?" Richard finally asked.

Rigot released Richard and stepped back, placing his hand on Richard's shoulder. "Yes! Of course! Come in, my friend! Have a seat!"

The apartment was dark and cluttered. Screens and indicators on multiple pieces of makeshift equipment projected red and blue light into the room, and tacked-up pieces of paper littered the walls with drawings, diagrams, and random notes as if Rigot was a detective trying to solve a homicide.

Rigot rushed to the sofa, picked up a pile of laundry, and moved it to the floor to make room for Richard and Aster to sit. Using his toes, he grabbed a pair of black shorts from the pile and tossed them upward, grabbing them out of the air with his right hand and sliding them on a second later.

Aster and Richard took a seat on the sofa.

Rigot sat backward on a small folding chair facing them. "So, my friend, as your building representative, I'm here to help you however I can. If you need something, you come to me. Day or night." He almost sounded like a respectable adult.

Richard felt somewhat comforted. "Thank you, Rigot. I appr—"

"Hey," Rigot said, giving up the charade and speaking with the excitement of an impatient child, "want to see something super neato I'm working on?"

"Sure. Why not?" Richard said, feeling he didn't have much choice in the matter.

An ecstatic Rigot dashed into the bedroom and returned a moment later with a disorganized pile of papers, tossing them onto an old filing cabinet at the edge of the sofa. He picked up a sheet from the pile and handed it to Richard. On the sheet were rough sketches of a small flying machine made of scrap materials. "This is my flying machine. I'm going to use it to get up to the door and back into GOD headquarters."

"Rigot!" Aster said in a furious tone. "We've talked about this! You can't build this. You know the rules. If we try to leave, we risk getting caught and endangering what we've built here. I need you to get this crazy idea out of your head!"

"Crazy?" he replied. "Do you know what is crazy to me? Lucifer has been gone for over a thousand years, and everyone else here is too idiotic to see it wasn't voluntary. Yes, yes, everyone talks about how he either left or is hiding, but if you knew him like I did, you'd understand he must have been kidnapped. He never would have gone back after what happened last time he tried."

"Not this again."

"Yes, 'this again,'" Rigot retorted. "I'm the only person who knows what happened last time because I'm the only one he trusted. Believe me: he'd never go back willingly."

Richard had been trying to stay out of this increasingly heated exchange, but his curiosity got the best of him. "What happened last time?"

Aster appeared shocked as she locked eyes with Rigot. "No. No. No. No. You can't tell him, Rigot. You need to keep that story to yourself."

"I'll shout it from the sky if I have to!" Rigot yelled, throwing his hands into the air. "You want to know what happened, my friend? I'll tell you." He began pacing the room.

"A few millennia after Lucifer was sent to Hell, he was called back by Joe. You see, Joe wanted to reconcile because he needed Lucifer's help. After the whole tree incident, Joe was having a difficult time controlling the new humans." Rigot paused. "Wait. Do you know the whole tree thing, or do I need to start over?"

Aster, who had dropped her head into her hands, gave what appeared to be an involuntary nod.

"Tree of Knowledge," Richard said. "Got Lucifer thrown into Hell. Here we are."

"Okay, good," Rigot said. "So the humans were doing all types of things Joe didn't approve of. He told Lucifer it felt like he was watching a runaway chain reaction; the infinite possibilities it presented posed too much risk to both his reputation and GOD. Joe has always been a man who needed to feel in control of his destiny, and the chaos of the free-willed humans had taken that from him."

"So," Richard said, "what did he need Lucifer for?"

"It was an act of desperation," Rigot replied. "Joe couldn't come up with a way to keep the humans under control without modifying the dimension's trajectory. He was hopeful that Lucifer could find a way to do it. But Lucifer was unwilling to help or change things again. He also didn't want to return to Hell. So he bought himself time by pitching terrible ideas he knew wouldn't work. Lucifer's hope was, given enough time, maybe Joe would come to appreciate the value of these humans and let it go. They could become friends again, and perhaps he'd let everyone out of the incinerator."

"That didn't happen, though, did it?" Richard asked, as his body shivered with nervous excitement.

"Sorry, my friend, it didn't. Over time, Joe grew more impatient and paranoid. Then one day he found a human—I believe his name was Norby or Nolan or something like that. Let's go with Norby. So Norby was naturally very compliant, and Joe saw this as an opportunity to reset the human population to one modeled around Norby. Joe began tampering with the dimension and gave Norby a vision to build a giant boat and fill it with two of every animal, and since Norby was exceptionally compliant, he did so. Joe then manipulated the climate and weather systems to flood the Earth, drowning all other life on the planet. Men, women, children, animals—all wiped out. Gone. Perished. Departed. Dead."

"Noah," Richard muttered as he recalled the familiar story from the Bible.

"No-ah?" Rigot replied. "Actually, *yes*-ah, my friend. And the worst part was they were all summarily tossed into the incinerator without even a chance to meet with an evaluator. The population of Hell skyrocketed overnight. The demons were overwhelmed. It was a disaster for both dimensions."

"That's horrible," Richard said. "But that seems like a win for Lucifer. The entire contents of Earth poured into his domain."

"One might think that," Rigot replied. "But at that point, Lucifer didn't care about Hell. He didn't consider it 'his domain.' Earth was the culmination of his life's work, what he truly cared about. To make matters worse, Joe managed to convince the board that the flood was Lucifer's doing. Seeing as he already had a history of modifying the trajectory and nothing like this had happened during his absence, it wasn't a hard leap to make. Some say having him as a fall guy was the point of bringing him back in the first place. But none of that mattered. By the time the board was aware of what happened, Lucifer had already made his way back to Hell, defeated and without hope for the future."

The frown on Aster's face matched her sullen posture. It was clear she was irritated.

Richard felt disoriented as he tried to piece the story together. "But then, how did humans still have free will afterward?"

"Turns out," Rigot answered, "compliance is a personal trait, a learned behavior, not something ingrained in the human genetic material, my friend. Norby was genetically the same as any other man and produced a lineage the same as any other human. All of those people perished because Joe confused nature with nurture."

Silence overtook the room as Richard absorbed everything he'd learned since going to Hell.

Rigot pointed toward the ceiling and stared upward, following the path of his index finger. "So. Who wants to help me build a flying machine?"

Chapter 10
Hope in a Box

Human cultures have an uncanny ability to assign absurd and often illogical connotations to words.

For example, the word "sex" is often seen as dirty and impolite, but sex itself is fun, pleasurable, and vitally important for the continuation of the species. Most people don't wish to discuss sex in any way, because culture has deemed it taboo, but a species doesn't get to the population of eight billion without a lot of people enjoying a lot of sex.

So what do humans do? They avoid the word. A female human would never invite her mother-in-law over for coffee and say, "Patricia, your son and I are having a lot of sex lately, which we both greatly enjoy, and it's started to pay dividends for the propagation of the species."

But she would say, "Patricia! Great news! You're going to be a grandmother!" Both are ways of saying the same thing, but the logical explanation for how Patricia became a grandmother is almost universally left out of such announcements in an attempt to avoid a word that is unfairly characterized as dirty.

Conversely, humans often ascribe positive meaning to words that frankly do not deserve such esteem.

"Hope" is one such word. Hope is a desire for something to happen in the future wrapped in a saccharin-sweet coating of faith. It could be the desire for a new job, desire for good health, or desire that your morbidly obese upstairs neighbor give up his new midnight cardio routine and return to a sedentary lifestyle. The concept of desire itself is seen as the path to suffering in many religions, but adding the "faith" qualifier transforms it into a virtue that humans will pay good money to have painted on cheap planks of wood and hung on the walls of their homes and cubicles.

Unfortunately, this is a lesson many humans must learn the hard way . . .

———

C *lara is forty-three,* Richard thought to himself as he lay huddled in his bed and stared at the exposed brick walls in his humble, poorly lit apartment on this chilly day in Gehenna, Hell. *Women live longer than men. I probably won't see her again for forty years. I won't see Sam or Tara for another seventy or eighty years. I guess I could get lucky, and someone could die young. Wow. I'm a terrible person. No wonder I'm in Hell.*

As is the nature of essential mechanical devices when we're at our most vulnerable, this was also the moment Richard's heater decided it had endured quite enough of his moping and committed suicide.

Not wanting to get out of bed and reveal to the underworld his red swollen eyes and the rash under his nostrils from wiping the mucus and salt water humans secreted when emotionally overwhelmed, Richard tried to put up with the encroaching cold as long as possible. But after hours of trying to pull himself together, he got up and meandered to Rigot's apartment to report the issue.

"Come in!" Rigot shouted after Richard knocked on his apartment door.

Richard opened the door and was immediately hit by a blast of air that was hot and humid enough to strike with the impact of a heavy, blunt object.

Inside he found Rigot bent over a pile of machine parts wearing nothing but a small blue Speedo. His derriere capped his long, spindly legs like a blueberry perched atop two well-balanced toothpicks.

"Damnit, Rigot!" Richard said, averting his gaze. "Do you ever wear pants?"

"Not unless I absolutely must, my friend. They limit my range of motion." Rigot took turns swinging each long, hairy leg in the air in a clockwise motion.

Richard had a much-needed laugh at Rigot's absurdity and lack of shame. On the outside, Richard had always been responsible, serious, and contemptuous of people like Rigot. But on the inside, he was envious and wished he had the same level of confidence in himself. "My heater is broken. How does this work? Are you the guy to fix it?"

"Yes, my friend," Rigot replied gently, with a look that made it clear he could tell that Richard had been weeping. "You can have one of my portable heaters until we can get yours fixed. Let me get it for you."

Rigot began to rearrange the piles of junk and machine parts in his apartment in search of the spare heater when he revealed a small stand supporting a television that looked exactly like the one Richard had watched in Peter's office. It was on, airing a show that appeared to be about some kind of family road trip.

"Goddamn it, Elaine!" an angry man growled through the television speakers. "If our exit was five miles ago, why are you telling me now? You have one job as the navigator! One job! I should have used the damn GPS."

"I didn't know we had TV in Hell," Richard said, amused at the show about the verbally abusive husband and his absent-minded wife.

"TV? What's TV?"

"That," Richard said, pointing at the screen. "I didn't know we had televisions or TV shows here."

"You mean my GOD box?"

"GOD box?" Richard asked, assuming the difference was primarily semantics.

"Yes, my friend, this isn't 'TV' or whatever you call it. It's an old device from GOD they threw down here. I turned it on, and all it did was show a bunch of black and white dots and lines and make *shhhh* sounds. Seemed like a useless machine to me, so I made it useful."

"Useful how?"

"Well, it's very complex to understand, but it does random calculations based on the probability of an infinite number of possible events that could take place within the GOD dimension and then shows the most probable results."

"So it makes up stories about things that may or may not be happening on Earth?"

"No. No. That'd be another useless machine, my friend. I don't create useless things. This machine presents what is probably happening in the GOD dimension within a ninety-nine-point-ninety-nine percent level of accuracy."

Richard fell silent as he thought through what Rigot had just said. "A virtual simulation of the physical simulation? That's amazing!" He stared into the screen.

"Amazing? Nah. This machine, to me, is a piece of garbage."

"Garbage?" Richard repeated, examining the box from all angles. "You've theoretically built a window into another dimension!"

"Yes, but what good is a window when you don't care what is on the other side? The GOD box shows random probable events, but I have no control over who the events pertain to or how long it continues the prediction for that subject. Every time I turn it off and back on, it predicts a new probable sequence of events for a new person in the GOD dimension. Therefore, if I wanted to use it to see what someone I care about is doing, such as Lucifer, I'd first have to be sure he's in the GOD dimension and then restart the box over and over, potentially billions of times, before it finally presented me with what he was probably doing, and even then, there's a point-zero-one percent chance it could be wrong."

Richard had an epiphany—one that required him to take control of the box and take it back to his apartment—but he'd never been much of a negotiator and was a lackluster liar at best. "You're right. That does sound like a worthless pile of garbage. Why even bother keeping it?" He felt about as believable as a B-movie actor.

"I don't know, my friend. It may be useful for parts someday, and it's somewhat heavy. Plus, it makes an excellent nightlight when I'm trying to find my way to the kitchen at night for a midnight snack."

"Ah, good point," Richard replied, a bit disappointed. "Hey, I have a decent lamp in my apartment, and that broken heater is full of parts. Why don't we make a trade? I'll give you the lamp and broken heater, and you give me this garbage box and the portable heater, and I won't bother you to fix my old heater?"

If Rigot knew the game Richard was playing, he certainly didn't let on. "My friend, I'll take your deal. Not that I have any use for your broken heater, but if it means I don't have to fix it and can spend more time on my flying machine, you have a deal."

An ecstatic Richard rushed past Rigot, unplugged the GOD box, picked it up, and dashed out the apartment door before Rigot could renege on their deal.

"Enjoy, my friend!" Richard heard Rigot shout down the hall as he closed his apartment door.

———

B ack at his apartment, Richard frantically plugged in the GOD box. He was overwhelmed with excitement that the very next image he could see on its screen might be that of Clara and the kids.

It wasn't that Richard didn't know the odds. He knew them all too well.

At three seconds per reset, assuming a unique person is simulated on every reset and there are almost 8,000,000,000 people on Earth, that's up to 24,000,000,000 seconds to scan them all, assuming no new people are born during the entire time. More people will be born though. It'll be longer. Not sure how to do that part.

In fact, the scale of the numbers bewildered Richard.

Okay, so 24,000,000,000 seconds divided by sixty seconds in a minute is 400,000,000 minutes. 400,000,000 minutes divided by sixty minutes in an hour is 6,666,667 hours. 6,666,667 hours divided by twenty-four hours in a day is 277,778 days. That's a lot of days.

But hope, like faith, wasn't rational, and its understanding of probability was nonexistent.

If we divide 277,778 days by 365 days in a year, we get 761 years. It could potentially take me 761 years of resetting this box without stopping before I see Clara on the screen. But she could just as easily be the very next face I see. I won't know unless I try.

Weeks passed as Richard turned the box on, saw an unfamiliar face, and immediately turned it off and on again. But as he jumped from one human experience to another, he would sometimes catch sight of something that wasn't his life but close enough.

He watched a young couple sit and talk for hours, getting to know one another, because it reminded him of his first date with Clara.

He watched a man in his late twenties just sit and talk with his father about how his life was going. His work, his relationships, his hopes and dreams. It made Richard regret he hadn't lived long enough to be there for those conversations with his children.

He watched an elderly widow grieve as she said goodbye to her husband of fifty years. He thought about how Clara might have experienced that same grief without him being there to comfort her.

As he watched, he realized how similar the other lives were to his own, and with the familiarity of each, he felt just a little closer to the life he had left behind, which was enough to sustain him as he continued resetting the box.

About two months after Richard began his obsession with the box, he heard a knock at the door.

"Richard! Are you there?" The voice belonged to Aster.

Richard hadn't seen Aster since his first day in Hell and was excited by the visit. "Coming!" he shouted.

He opened the door and welcomed Aster inside his sparsely furnished apartment, giving her a friendly hug.

"Hey, stranger," Aster said. "I was in the area, and it hit me that I hadn't seen you in a while, so I figured I'd drop in and see how you're holding up."

"I'm good," he said. "I'm really good." He nodded—too long, he realized—and smiled what he knew was an unconvincing smile.

Aster looked Richard up and down. "You sure don't look good," she said, with a hint of disgust. "You do know we have toiletries and shaving supplies in Hell, right?"

"Yeah, sorry," Richard said. "I've been very busy lately."

"Oh, that's great to hear. What have you been doing?"

Richard tried to come up with a cover story, but he wasn't that quick-witted. "You know, a little of this, a little of that."

From the bedroom came the raspy voice of an angry old man, who yelled, "One hundred bucks for an oil change? What kind of scam is this?" The words echoed off the apartment's hardwood floors and high ceilings.

Aster looked surprised. "What was that? Is someone else here?"

"I don't know what you're talking about," Richard said, unable to hide the look of culpability on his face.

Aster grew silent, listening.

"I don't care what other shops would charge! This is highway robbery! You wait until I get home! I know how to use the internets! I'll put this place out of business!"

Aster furrowed her brows in confusion. "You don't hear that irrationally angry man yelling in your bedroom?"

Realizing he wasn't going to be able to continue pretending to be either daft or deaf, Richard dropped the act. "Oh, you mean my television. It was a gift from Rigot."

"How do you have television?" Aster asked. "We don't have any broadcasts here."

"Are . . . are you sure?" Richard replied. "Maybe we do, and you just didn't get the announcement or something."

Aster squinted and raised one eyebrow in suspicion. She walked into the back bedroom and stared at the box. "What's this show?"

"Oh, um, it's one of my favorites. *Angry . . . Angry Adam.* Yes, *Angry Adam.* It's a show about an old man who's unhappy with his life."

"That'd be all of them! Am I right?" Aster joked. She continued watching. "It sure has an improvisational tone to it, doesn't it?"

"Yeah, I guess it makes it feel more real."

"What did you say the show was called again?"

"*Angry Adam,*" Richard replied, proud that he had committed that part of the story to memory.

"I wonder why it's called that. The mechanic just called him Steve."

Richard began to dig himself deeper. "Well, he goes by Adam but sometimes Steve, but *Angry Steve* didn't have the same ring, I suppose."

"Sounds like lazy writing to me," Aster said. "Hard to believe. All of the best writers are here in Hell." Aster made a startled-yet-puzzled face, as if she had been unexpectedly struck by a wet sock. "Richard, this looks like Earth. We don't have oil changes here in Hell. We don't even have cars, for that matter."

Richard started to think of his next fabrication, but by this point, he had grown tired of lying to Aster and knew he couldn't keep up the charade. "Okay, so it's a TV that broadcasts what's happening in the GOD dimension—at least, what it *thinks* is happening. I'm sorry. It's just . . ."

Aster's eyes widened with a look of realization. "So you look like Old Hell, you smell like rotten cabbage, and you have a box that shows you the GOD dimension. Have you been in here mindlessly watching this thing and dreaming of home?"

"Yes! That's it! You've caught me." He didn't want to explain how he constantly reset it in his search for Clara. Somehow, this lie was less embarrassing.

Aster looked Richard in the eyes and spoke in a tone of sincere concern. "Richard, I've been doing this demon thing for a long time. I know what homesickness and grief do to a person. This isn't healthy."

"I know, I know," Richard said in a dismissive tone.

Aster was clearly trying to avoid lecturing Richard, so she tried another tactic. "You want to go to Hell of a Cup? You love that place, and it'll get you out of the house. Maybe we can take a nice walk through the gardens afterward? We can catch up."

Richard peered at the box and thought about how many billion resets he still had to make. "I really appreciate the offer, but no thanks. Maybe another time."

"Come on," she said. "We can bring the TV with us!" She rushed over and playfully started pushing the wheeled cart, not realizing the box was plugged into the wall.

"No! Don't!" Richard shouted, but he was too late.

As the box reached the end of its cord, it fell off the cart and landed on the floor with a sudden and deafening crash.

"No! No! No!" Richard rushed over to the box lying on the floor. "Look what you've done!"

The screen was shattered.

Richard felt a pain in his stomach and a lump in his throat. He dropped to his knees and began looking the box over in hopes of repairing it, but he didn't know what he was looking at. He'd never been particularly handy. "You ruined it!" he yelled. "It was all I had, and you ruined it!"

Chapter 11
Good Grief

"I 'll miss you, but it's time we part," Richard said to the yellow balloon as he held it out the thirteenth-floor window of the Gehenna Grief Management Center.

A modest building by Hell standards, with pink and purple glass that made the minimalist white interior feel warm and soft, the Grief Management Center looked like something between a hospital and a modern art museum.

The balloon had hair of black yarn glued to the top and a smiling face drawn on it with a permanent marker and the name *Clara* written along the bottom.

Richard was reluctant to part with the balloon, both because he had made it to symbolize the wife and family he had left behind and because he had spent the better part of the afternoon making it and was quite proud of his workmanship.

"Very good!" cheered the group therapy leader, a handsome and energetic young gentleman with blue eyes and messy blond hair who went by Dr. Gregg. "Now, say, 'I'm going to move on now, and I'll see you again one day soon. I love you, and I know you love me.'"

Richard followed the instructions and repeated the words to his balloon.

He was joined by roughly thirty other participants completing the weeklong grief counseling boot camp designed to help the damned who struggled with letting go of their past lives. This boot camp was recommended for all new inhabitants of Hell, but most refused treatment, choosing to manage their own grief, often ineffectively. Richard was attending as a favor to Aster.

"Okay now!" an overly enthusiastic Dr. Gregg shouted, while clapping his hands together. "Let's count down to release our grief! On the count of three, we're all going to let go of our grief and watch it float away! One!"

Sounds like pop psychology quackery to me, thought Richard as he prepared to release the balloon.

"Two!"

I can't believe this guy had his own daytime talk show. No wonder he's in Hell.

"Three!"

Okay, guess this is goodbye.

Richard released his balloon on cue and watched it float away.

He felt no better. Honestly, he was even a bit more grieved having just lost a perfectly nice balloon.

"Goodbye, grief!" Dr. Gregg shouted as everyone clapped. "See you later! *Ciao! Sayonara! Arrivederci!*"

At the end of the session, Dr. Gregg approached each patient lined up along the wall of open windows and spoke with them briefly to assess their mental state and wish them well.

When he approached Richard, he placed his hand on Richard's shoulder, looked into his eyes, and asked genuinely, "How do you feel? Better?"

Richard didn't want to crush the spirit of such an optimistic and positive person, so he did what the other thirtyish participants did and lied. "Yes. I feel so much better. Like a weight has been lifted."

"Excellent!" the doctor exclaimed. "You're free to go home and enjoy your afterlife to the fullest!"

"Thank you, Doctor."

The doctor gave him an oversized grin. "Oh! Before you go, I have a gift for you!"

"Oh really? You didn't have to do that." For a moment, Richard felt guilty for perhaps judging the doctor too harshly.

Dr. Gregg reached into his coat, pulled out a book, and handed it to Richard. On the cover was a picture of the doctor in a white coat leaning up against a wall while biting on the earpiece of a pair of glasses. To the right of the doctor was the title, *Grief to Great: How I Got Beyond Death and You Can Too!* in bold red letters.

Richard tried to be polite but couldn't hide the disappointment on his face. "Oh, wow, thank you. Like I said, you really didn't need to give me a gift."

"No, silly!" the doctor said. "The book isn't the gift. The knowledge *in* the book is the gift. The book itself costs fifty credits, and I already had it charged to your account. Enjoy!"

By now, Richard wanted to tell the doctor what he really thought of this "gift"—if he could even call it that—but before he could get the words out, Dr. Gregg moved on to the next participant.

Defeated and thoroughly frustrated with the entire process, Richard gathered his belongings and shuffled toward the exit. As he passed a trash can, he tossed Dr. Gregg's book inside and emptied the contents of a half-empty coffee cup atop it, staining and deforming the cover.

I hope he sees it sitting in that pile of trash where it belongs.

Upon opening the exit door, he saw Aster patiently waiting for him outside. She wore her long black hair in a ponytail and sported a green sundress with a brown knit cardigan to counteract the weather, which was a perfect combination of breezy and cool. "Richard! Over here!" she shouted, with an exaggerated wave that swung from one side of her body to the other. "Mind if I walk you back to your apartment? It's such a beautiful day, and I really wanted to catch up."

"Absolutely!" Richard replied, with a smile, excited to see a familiar face.

They walked along the shore of Jacobia Lake, Gehenna's largest freshwater reservoir and fed by the River Styx. The lake was encircled in rings of red roses and apple trees that made for hours of meandering, the walking paths slowly leading visitors outside the center of town.

"So," Aster said, "how was Dr. Gregg? He's really something, right?"

"Yeah, something." Richard turned to stare at a large blue building in the distance to avoid eye contact with Aster.

"What's wrong, Richard?"

"It's nothing. Forget I said anything."

Aster stepped in front of Richard, stopped, and turned to face him. "Richard, it's my job to see to it you adapt well. I need honesty."

He wanted to complain about his ineffective grief treatment but in typical midwestern fashion felt the need to be asked twice after first denying there was an issue before he could voice any complaint. "Fine. Dr. Gregg was a quack who did nothing but force us to talk about our feelings in a big kumbaya circle and make pathetic and time-consuming symbolic handcrafts. But if I'd told him he was just an ineffective asshole, then *I* would have been the asshole because he was such a nice person. So instead, I had to spend a week listening to thirty other people talk about their sob stories and glue yarn to random objects. Cups, balloons—at one point, he made us glue yarn to our own right hands and talk to them."

Aster laughed. "He made you talk with your own hand? Did you have to answer back?" She turned her right hand into a small mouth with her thumb and index finger. "Hello, Richard! Do you feel *saaaad* today?" the hand asked, as Aster spoke out of the corner of her mouth.

Richard chuckled with Aster. "Yes! It was exactly like that! But you need a lot more markers and yarn."

"I'm *so* sorry you had to do that, Richard. I mean, you probably have *so* much to do in Hell, like sitting around your apartment resetting boxes over and over. A busy man like you shouldn't have to waste his precious time trying to manage grief in a productive manner so he can enjoy exploring the beautiful gardens, libraries, and museums of Gehenna. It isn't like you have an eternity of time to waste."

Richard picked up on the sarcasm, "Okay, okay. Fair enough." He chuckled once more before changing the subject. "You mentioned libraries and museums. You know, when I was zoning out listening to the twenty-fifth sob story, I started to think about time. When I was alive, I wanted to be a scholar and write a book, but I never had the time. I was too busy working and raising a family. Maybe that's what I'll do with my time."

"That's a fantastic idea, Richard!" Aster exclaimed, beaming with delight. "Yes, there are many libraries and museums in Hell, especially here in the city of Gehenna. After all, history's greatest minds were tossed into Hell for being inherently uncontrollable. The two largest collections here are Gehenna Gallery and Belial Bibliotheca. Gehenna

Gallery contains artifacts from Old Hell, exhibits about the building of New Hell by the Bezalel Brotherhood, and art by some of the greatest artists who ever lived, died, and were tossed into Hell. The Belial Biblio contains the full history of Earth and Hell, written by those who experienced it first-hand, as well as the recorded discoveries and creations of every writer, scientist, inventor, or scholar ever cast into Hell."

"Scholar?" he said. "If I wrote my book, maybe it could be in the library one day?"

"Absolutely! I can see it now! *The History of Some Such Thing* by Richard Wilkins."

Richard was filled with purpose at the prospect of finally achieving his lifelong dream of having a book placed on the shelves of a library he hadn't known existed five minutes ago. "Then that's what I'll do. I'll write a book. You know, I feel better already. Maybe you should write a book, *Get Over Grief: How to Distract Yourself from Your Pain* by Dr. Aster."

"Thanks," she said, "but I'm much too busy actually helping people to waste my time writing about helping people."

"Oh, eternity isn't enough time for you?" he said in a mocking tone. "You probably have so much to do in Hell, like sitting around your apartment and blah, blah, blah."

"Shut up, Richard," she said, her face red with embarrassment.

Richard was enjoying the moment when suddenly he felt what he thought was a large spider land on his head. "What the hell? Spider! Get it off!" He shook his head wildly, but the spider wouldn't relent. With each shake, it felt like the spider was embedding itself further into his hair.

Aster reached over and grabbed the spider by one of its legs and held it in the air in front of Richard's face. The spider had dozens of long black stringy legs and a yellow abdomen.

"My grief balloon!" Richard bellowed, with delight. "It came back to me!"

She placed the deflated balloon and yarn on her right hand like a wig and once again spoke from the mouth made by her thumb and index finger. "See, Richard! Things are already looking up!"

Chapter 12
Belial Biblio

H umans often do things that seem illogical to an outsider, like cramming their slobbery food holes together and forcing bacteria-laced saliva into each other's digestive tract as a form of romantic affection. If you were to ask them why they do such things, they'd usually reply with, "I don't know. Guess we've just always done it that way."

What they truly mean is that this custom has been done for a sufficient number of generations that no one really knows when it started. This could be as little as two or three generations, because it simply needs to be long enough for anyone alive to have no memory of a time before the absurd custom became commonplace or be too old to be taken seriously when they argue otherwise.

But as Richard would soon find out, this dynamic of human memory works similarly in an environment where generations pile up *ad infinitum* and some have memories that go back centuries . . .

———

"**E**xcuse me, sir," Richard whispered.

"Yes?" replied Aeschylus, the gaunt elderly head librarian of the prestigious Belial Bibliotheca.

The Belial Bibliotheca—Belial Biblio for short—was a gargantuan library with clear and emerald-green glass windows placed upon substantial hand-hewn post-and-beam wood supports and wrought-iron framing that enclosed the sprawling building in the style of an enormous Victorian conservatory. Only three stories tall, it spanned five city blocks, and its collections filled another several subterranean levels. The three above-ground floors opened around a central atrium containing desks, a small garden, and wrought-iron staircases leading from the atrium to each level and shorter staircases between each level at certain convenient intervals.

Richard stood at the center of the atrium, leaning over a large bronze desk with a sign that read *Information* hanging above it. "Can you tell me where to find the history books?"

"Of course," Aeschylus whispered, raising a wrinkled and shaky hand and pointing to an area behind Richard. "Go up to the third floor. Very back right corner. You'll see a sign for *Personal Health*, and there you should find what you're looking for."

Personal Health? Richard thought. *This must be one of those quirky Hell things, like teapots and tarts or whatever.*

Richard made the trek up the nearest iron staircase to the third floor and then walked the quarter mile to the back right corner in search of the Personal Health section. As he wandered the shelves, he found titles such as *Self-Care: How to Avoid Burnout in Hell, Digestive Damnation, and Hellish Health Hacks.* However, there were no titles that indicated any of the books pertained to history.

Why does everyone in the afterlife give bad directions? Richard wondered.

As he turned the corner into the Personal Fitness section, he saw the back of a tall and lanky man wearing a stained white tank top and blue cutoff shorts that were one size too small. The man had long black hair and was doing what appeared to be repetitions of squats and lunges while staring at a slight reflection of himself in the emerald glass window.

"Rigot?"

"My friend!" Rigot yelped with pure delight. He broke from his morning exercise routine and rushed over to give Richard another one of his awkward embraces. "What are you doing here?"

Richard tried to answer, but it came out as more of a muffled murmur due to his mouth being covered by Rigot's hairy exposed chest. *"Mmm mmr mm rrr ar ar rerere reme."*

"History?" Rigot replied, somehow able to translate Richard's garbled response into words. "That's way on the opposite end of the library. What are you doing all the way over here?"

"I know," Richard said, with a grunt, as he wedged his arms between his chest and Rigot's stomach, pushing himself free. "The librarian sent me here, but I don't know why."

Rigot stopped for a moment, gave the idea some thought, and began to laugh. "Aeschylus is hard of hearing, my friend! Centuries of working in a quiet library atrophied his eardrums. I bet he thought you said hysterectomy!"

"Of course, he did," Richard replied, at this point expecting no less of a preposterous explanation.

"History, huh? What kind of history books are you looking for?"

"I'm not sure yet. I want to write a history book, but I don't know what would be needed at this library. I was thinking something about eighteenth-century Spanish history. It was my college major."

Rigot chided him. "Are you Spanish, my friend?"

"No."

"Did you live in the eighteenth century?"

"No."

"Do you realize how many eighteenth-century Spanish souls are here in Hell?"

"Not really, but I don't see how that's relevant."

"Millions, my friend, and many of them have already written firsthand accounts that make up the shelves of the history section. Many of them are truly fantastic memoirs of the time and place. My personal favorite is one man's story of *cacafuego*."

"That was the sixteenth century," Richard retorted, pleased with himself.

"Not the boat, my friend. This was about an overly spicy *paella*." Rigot stopped and grinned, waiting for a laugh from Richard that would never come. "My point is, if you want to write something worthy of these shelves, you need to write something no one else has written."

"And how do you suggest I do that?" Richard asked, with a hint of skepticism in his voice. "Maybe I should tell my story?"

"Your life? What would that be? The story of a man who led a boring life, then died? Ninety-nine percent of the people here could write that book."

Richard felt his face burn red as he glared at Rigot.

"I'm sorry, my friend. That was low and mean. I got carried away."

"It's okay," Richard said. "It hurts, but you aren't wrong. I doubt a story about a guy who spent his life just screwing and banging all day long will hold anyone's interest."

Rigot paused for a moment, no doubt thinking maybe he

had been too quick to judge Richard's life. He shook off the thought and continued. "Look, my friend, what you need is a history that everyone cares about, told from an angle no one has taken before, and I know just the thing."

Richard perked up with excitement. "And what would that be?"

Rigot scanned their immediate surroundings as if to make sure no one else was listening. "Did you know that less than one percent of the inhabitants of Hell ever laid eyes on Lucifer? He left thousands of years ago. Most of the people here arrived after he left. When he *was* here, he usually kept to himself, only making contact through demons and close friends like me. If you go out on the street today and ask anyone if they truly believe he ever existed, the majority will tell you he was some government-contrived boogeyman whose pending return was designed to keep people in line."

"That seems hard to believe," Richard said, "given the story Aster told me. People don't think he ever really existed?"

"Would you? Imagine being told for over a thousand years he could come back any day and you never see him. Eventually you'd lose faith too. When I try to tell people he's real, they tell me I'm just part of the conspiracy and treat me like a crazy person."

"I see what you mean," Richard muttered. "So what do you propose?"

"My friend, I'm a brilliant inventor, a gifted philosopher, and by all accounts an amazing lover, but my writing is just so-so. What if I gave my story to you? You come by my apartment, help me work on my flying machine, and while we work, I'll share with you everything I know about Lucifer. By the time we're done, I'll have my flying machine and you'll have a book that everyone in Gehenna will want to read."

Richard spoke in a whisper to ensure no one would overhear him. "This sounds great, Rigot, really great, but isn't the flying machine illegal?"

"No! Of course not, my friend!" yelled Rigot, completely disregarding Richard's discretion. "The flying machine is perfectly legal. *Flying it to the door of the incinerator* is illegal. Very illegal, in fact. But building a flying machine for recreational use? That's absolutely legal."

"What about Aster?" Richard asked. "She seems to think the flying machine is a terrible idea."

"She is a demon, my friend. They're required to say things like that. It's their job. She's only covering her glass."

"You mean covering her ass?"

"Ass, glass—the point is, she's required to say that. If I'm successful in finding Lucifer, she'll be the first in line to thank me. They were close friends. She loved him like I do."

"So," Richard said, giving Rigot a knowing look, "I help you build this 'recreational flying machine,' and in exchange, you'll help me write the full history of Lucifer?"

"Exactly, my friend! Do we have a deal?"

Richard stopped for a moment to survey the vast library's halls and the millennia's worth of collective works. His thoughts filled with visions of strangers coming up to him on the streets, telling him how much they loved his book and how his writing had changed their lives. He imagined himself making witty banter on Hell's speaker circuit, discussing his scholarly research process. He could see it all as clear as day. He was sold. "We have a deal," he said, reaching out to shake Rigot's hand.

Rigot stepped past Richard's extended hand for yet another awkward embrace. "Excellent, my friend! I'll see you tomorrow! Bright and early!"

Chapter 13
Chaos and Flying Machines

"Come in!" Rigot shouted, after Richard knocked on his apartment door.

Upon opening the door, Richard found Rigot wearing properly fitting pants, which struck Richard as odd, but he wasn't quite sure why.

"Where do you want to start, my friend?" Rigot asked, ushering Richard inside with his left arm while staring at a pile of parts and broken office equipment.

"I've no clue," Richard replied. "This is your flying machine."

"No, my friend, I mean in Lucifer's story. Where would you like me to start?"

"Oh, I don't know. I guess at the beginning."

"The beginning. That's always a good place to start, my friend." Rigot pointed to a heap of old office equipment in the corner. "Okay, you start breaking apart these old phones and copy machines. Take out any copper wire and magnets you find and place them in separate piles. While you do that, I'll start at the beginning."

Richard retrieved a small pen and notebook from his front pocket to begin taking notes. Truth be told, he figured he probably didn't need the notes, but his vision of scribbling shorthand in the small notebook like a reporter for the local paper made him feel more legitimate as a writer.

"No, my friend," Rigot objected. "You need your hands for this." He handed Richard a small red metal toolbox. "Use your hands to work and your ears and brain to listen."

Richard sorted through the box of tools and spotted a hammer, screwdrivers, wire cutters, and an assortment of other tools. "Screwing and banging—well, unscrewing and smashing in this case—I think I can handle that."

"Very good, my friend," Rigot replied. "So. The beginning. The first thing I need you to do is forget everything you've heard thus far about Lucifer and Joe. The video we all had to watch at GOD is only one side of a story, and what Aster is required to tell you is another, but two half-truths don't always make a whole one."

"Got it." Richard unscrewed the fasteners from the bottom of an old office phone.

"Okay, so the beginning. To understand Lucifer, you must first understand how he relates to Joe. And to understand that, you must understand their beginnings." Rigot began disassembling a broken TV with a screwdriver. "Lucifer came from an affluent family. They built their fortune processing the soft worthless metal of gold into a harder alloy that could be used for road pavement. He wanted for nothing but was always wanting. He was surrounded by beauty, and his parents never wished for him to experience pain, so they sheltered him, shielding him from seeing the ugliness of the world. That's where his obsession with beauty comes from. He was an adult when he left his family's compound and saw all of the pain and suffering in the world for the first time, but rather than feeling empathy for those who were suffering, he felt disgust. In the eyes of Lucifer, to strive for beauty was to strive for normalcy."

"So he was always discontented?" Richard asked. "I imagine consistent beauty is very difficult to achieve."

"Yes, when he could achieve beauty, he was happy and excited. But when he couldn't and had to face the banality of the real world, he was brooding and restless. That was why his parents agreed to buy him his first observable dimension—so he could fill it with all the beauty he wanted and live in a fantasy."

"They bought it for him?" Richard asked. "I thought he found it?"

"No, my friend. Lucifer was much too impetuous for that."

"What about Joe?" Richard asked, as he cut away the copper wires inside the disassembled phone and set them aside in a pile. "I was told he found his first void as a young man. I can only assume he too came from a well-to-do family?"

"What did I tell you about forgetting everything you were told?" Rigot asked. "No, he didn't come from a good family. He didn't come from any family, for that matter. He was an orphan. Based on the stories Lucifer told me about him, his upbringing was painful chaos. Jumping from orphanage to orphanage. He'd form close relationships with other kids, and they'd be adopted, abandoning him at the orphanage and leaving him for a life he could only dream of. He was treated like he was nothing. Never had anyone to hold on to or love him in return. Lucifer always figured that was why Joe was so obsessed with being in control. For him, chaos was always pain, and control meant comfort, however fleeting. Joe never wanted to fall back to that pain again and felt the only way he could do that was by controlling his own destiny, which is exactly what he did. He worked hard, bought an older-model observable dimension mining kit, mined day and night for years, trying to find his way out of poverty, and then one day, the favored sibling of chaos—luck—showed her face, and Joe found his first void and made a name for himself."

"Wow," Richard said. "So they really are complete opposites in every way."

Rigot gave Richard a condescending look. "What? Is that what you got from that story, my friend? Were you not listening?"

Richard felt a bit flustered. "I'm sorry, but you said—"

"They may have *started* at different points, but what fuels them both is the same: normalcy. A want for normalcy and comfort. For Lucifer, that normalcy looks like the ubiquitous beauty of his upbringing. For Joe, that normalcy looks like a life where he never has to go back to the pain he once knew. One man is running toward something, while the other is running away from something, but they're both running toward the same end point. In my mind, they're the same."

"I suppose that makes sense." Richard tossed the empty plastic shell of the telephone over his shoulder. "But I thought Lucifer was about chaos? Something about chaos and beauty, according to Aster."

Rigot gave Richard a look that indicated he had broken the rules yet again by referencing Aster's story. "Chaos, in that context, simply means a lack of control. Random chance. People misunderstand chaos. When random chance leads to undesirable results, we call it chaos, but when it leads to beneficial outcomes, we call it luck or blessings, but it's the same force: random probability acting with minimal control. It's neither good nor evil. But while control means comfort and safety—concepts humans relate with positive things—it can also mean suppression and oppression. Likewise, chaos means pain and potential for more pain, but it can also mean freedom and creativity. In a controlled environment, if you wanted to create beauty, you'd have to control how beauty is created and have a near-infinite number of recipes to create all of the beauty that chaos creates on its own."

"So," Richard said, a bit confused, "chaos is beauty?"

"No. Chaos isn't beauty. Chaos has no such characteristics. But look at Earth's universe, the random galaxies and celestial bodies chaotically exploding and smashing into each other and reforming continuously. When you look out at it, it's so beautiful. Sure, there are some basic rules in the laws of physics, but most of the beauty of the universe is created by letting these forces interact in uncontrolled ways and seeing what comes out the other end. These near-infinite possible reactions often lead to undesirable things as well, such as the destruction of entire solar systems, but they also create a lot of beauty a thinking mind wouldn't consider taking the steps to create."

"I'm sorry," Richard said, as he tried to pry a magnet out of a headset. "I'm not following you."

Rigot stopped and stared at the ceiling, a look of concentration overtaking his face. "Okay, so let's say you and your family left for a nice vacation. Right? And while you're gone, your house burns down. How would you feel about that?"

"I'd be pretty upset. In that case, chaos did something objectively terrible and ugly."

"But did it?" Rigot countered. "Had you and your family been home—perhaps asleep in your beds—when the fire happened, some or all of you could have perished. The random chance that the cause of the fire happened while you were out on vacation could have been one of the best things that ever happened to you and led to millions of beautiful new memories that may never have existed had chaos not struck when it did. Same chaos, same event. Looked at one way, it's ugly and terrible, but from another, it's a beautiful blessing. No one would think beauty could be created that way, but the universe has a way of doing things in ways we just can't predict."

Richard was quiet for a moment as he pondered Rigot's points. "So Lucifer doesn't enjoy chaos but sees it as a means to an end in creating beauty?"

"Yes," Rigot replied. "Exactly. Since he had always seen the beauty created by chaos but had never personally felt its painful sting, his frame of reference for the nature of chaos was skewed."

"Ah." Richard used a magnet from the phone to test the attractive properties of other metals nearby. "And Joe—he sees the inherently risky part of chaos, and his attempts at control are really just him trying his best to spare himself and others pain?"

"You've got it, my friend," Rigot said, with a smile that indicated his satisfaction.

"So if I'm following you, neither man is inherently good or bad. Both are just acting in ways that help them reach their desired end, which they separately feel is best, based on their own past experiences."

Rigot picked up a hammer and began smashing through the glass on a copy machine. "To understand this is to understand why Lucifer and Joe were destined to be partners!" he shouted over the noise of breaking glass. "Two men who only care about the ends—and not the means to those ends—are destined to fail because they're willing to ignore any problems or discard any issues that get in their way. But working together, they force one another to consider the means and, in doing so, avoid those problems. They balance one another out. That's why Lucifer approached Joe to team up on GOD."

"Wait," Richard said. "I thought Joe approached Lucifer?"

Rigot turned and gave him a stern look. "What do I keep telling you? Forget everything you know! That's the official line of the demons. They want it to seem like Lucifer saved Joe. Both men's companies were flailing, but do you really think Joe just got lucky twice in finding another void? The truth is Lucifer's parents bought him another and commanded him not to ruin it this time with a bunch of beautiful but useless five-headed rainbow dragons and purple turtles that shit gumdrops."

"Interesting," Richard muttered as he peered over at Rigot's rough plans for the flying machine atop the nearby file cabinet. "Mind if I ask you an unrelated question?"

"Sure, my friend, ask away."

"So this flying machine. It's supposed to be like an airplane, right? A glider with a motor?"

"Yes, my friend, that's the basic concept."

"Okay, and you have to take it up to the door just above the clouds, correct?"

"Correct."

"Okay, that's what I thought," Richard said. "If it has to glide to stay in the air, how do you plan to stop it when you reach the door? Since the door is straight above the trampoline, wouldn't something simpler like a hot air balloon be easier and more effective?"

Rigot stopped for a moment and gave the idea some thought. He glanced around the room at the piles of wire, magnets, broken glass, and empty plastic electronics cases. "Shit! Dammit! Son of a bitch!" he screamed and started to smash random objects with his hammer.

Richard backed away and covered his face to avoid the shrapnel that was being scattered around the small apartment. In admiring Rigot's brilliance, he had forgotten he was still a madman. "I'm sorry I said anything!" he shouted over the cacophony, trying to calm Rigot.

Rigot stopped and turned to Richard, trembling and out of

breath. "No, my friend, don't be sorry. You just saved me months of work. I'm not mad at you. I'm mad at myself. I got so lost in thinking about the end, I never stopped to consider the means."

"Happens to the best of us," Richard said, with a smile.

Chapter 14
A Bountiful Bezalel

"'**B**ezalel! Oh, Bezalel! You brought us comfort in Hell!'" Rigot sang as he danced around his apartment, lighting candles and setting out small sugary treats.

Hell had two seasons: a perfectly bright, breezy, and sometimes chilly season called Anoixi that lasted precisely eighteen Earth months, followed by Psychros, a sudden and brutally cold and snowy period that lasted roughly two months, sometimes more, sometimes less. The nights were long during Psychros, and the days were short, often to the point of seeming nonexistent.

As humans did every year on the Psychros solstice, the longest and coldest night of the year, the inhabitants of Hell celebrated the light in the darkness. They called this holiday Bezalel in honor of the Bezalel Brotherhood and the work they had done and the pain they had endured to turn Hell from fire and torment into an ideal metropolis.

Richard sat at a nearby workstation, fidgeting with a homemade sewing machine Rigot had hastily assembled from parts originally salvaged for the flying machine. For months, Richard had been responsible for sewing the seams of the hot air balloon envelope, while Rigot had focused on building a collapsible basket, a lightweight burner, and a large cart for transporting the entire project to and from his apartment.

Richard looked up as Rigot twirled around him and placed a small chocolate candy at his workstation. "Who're the sweets for?"

Rigot appeared absolutely giddy. "Democritus! The cheerful philosopher! Every Bezalel, Democritus visits every household in Hell and devours sweets, and for those who have been good, he grants one wish."

"Oh, so kind of like Santa Claus then?" Richard asked.

"No!" Rigot corrected him. "This is nothing like your confusing holiday that's somehow about both the birth of a man your culture believes to be their Messiah and a morbidly obese elf that brings your children cheap plastic sweatshop garbage. On Bezalel, the wish can be for yourself or for someone else. It doesn't have to be stuff. Legend says Democritus shrinks down to the size of a single atom, floats up your nostrils while you're sleeping, and reads your mind so he knows your heart's utmost desires. If you're found worthy, he grants your wish."

"Well," Richard mused, "that seems oddly heartwarming."

"What is it you wish for, my friend? What do you wish for this Bezalel?"

"I haven't given it much thought. You just told me about this ten seconds ago. But I guess my wish would be what it's been for months: to see Clara and the kids again." Richard felt a small amount of salt water welling up in his left eye. He locked his gaze onto the piece of balloon he was stitching to avoid making eye contact with Rigot.

"That's a good wish, my friend. A little selfish, but not *too* selfish. Right where a wish should be. I hope Democritus grants it for you."

"Thanks, Rigot. What is it you wish for?"

"Oh, I can't tell you, my friend. If I do, it won't come true!"

"Wait. What?" Richard chuckled. "You just asked me what my wish was, and I told you, so now mine won't come true?"

"Yep," Rigot replied, with a trickster's smile. "Those are the rules, my friend. We all learned that one the hard way on our first Bezalel."

"I bet I know what it is anyway," Richard said. "Do you get your wish if I say what it is?"

"No! Don't say it, my friend! You'll ruin it!"

"Hey, what's fair is fair," Richard said, with a faux maniacal laugh. "You did it to me. "You wish to find Lu—"

"Shut up! Shut up! Lalalalala!" Rigot stuck his fingers in his ears, bouncing around the room like a small child that had enjoyed one too many Bezalel sweets.

"Okay, okay," Richard reassured him. "I won't say it out loud."

"Thank you, my friend. I know it's a silly superstition, but I've asked for it every year for the past several millennia and haven't had anyone spoil it yet."

"Well, I have some good news for you," Richard said, looking up from the balloon.

"Is it done?" Rigot asked, still bouncing around with excitement.

"Yes, it's done." Richard held up a small corner of the balloon.

"Excellent! Let's take it out for a test spin!"

"Test spin?" Richard asked. "It's absolutely freezing out there."

"That's the best time to fly a hot air balloon! The temperature difference between the inside and outside of the balloon will be at its greatest, which will create more lift!" Rigot spun around the room, pointing toward the ceiling. "Plus! I can show you what Gehenna looks like from the sky on Bezalel. All the buildings will have candles lit, and the streets will be lined with lights. To see it all from the sky will be glorious! I bet we could even hear people singing! 'Bezalel, Oh Bezalel! This is our story to tell! Bezalel! Oh Bezalel! You brought us comfort in Hell!'"

Rigot's sense of wonder was contagious.

"Screw it. Let's do it," Richard declared, knowing it would make his friend happy.

"Great! Let's get this giant balloon loaded into the cart with the basket and see if we can make it downstairs to the courtyard without getting stuck!"

It took over an hour to make it to the courtyard with the cart, which wanted to tip over at every turn and wedge itself into every doorway of the apartment building, but eventually, after jammed fingers, sore backs, and a more-than-generous sprinkling of profanity, they made it to the courtyard.

Within an hour of reaching the courtyard, they had the balloon set up and ready to take off. Snow fell and danced in the wind. The cold air bit Richard's nose and hands, making the heat from the burner all the more pleasurable as he climbed into the basket.

"Are you ready?" Rigot asked.

"I suppose I'm as ready as I can be," Richard replied. "It's not like I can die again."

"Yes, my friend. It's funny how being unafraid of death lets us feel free to live. Okay. Enough chitchat. Here we go!" Rigot pulled on the cord of the burner, releasing more gas to expand the flame and send the balloon slowly meandering into the air.

As they ascended, they caught a steady wind that carried them over the center of Gehenna.

"Look down there, my friend! In the snow!" Rigot pointed to a display the size of a blue whale in the city park. "Do you see the candles arranged into the shape of an open hand?"

"Yeah! I see it!" Richard cried, with the excitement of a child.

"That's the symbol for the Bezalel Brotherhood. The hand serves as a reminder of the bare hands they thrust into the flames to turn over the ash and smother the fires of Hell. It's to remind us that, no matter how painful, we have the power to make a better world for ourselves and those that come after us."

"That's really beautiful," Richard said. "Look at the Belial Biblio! It's glowing like a giant green emerald!"

"Yes, my friend. They light thousands of candles in the Belial on Bezalel. I've always questioned the wisdom of that much fire sharing space with that much wood and paper, but they've done it every year for centuries without issue. It's enough to make anyone believe in Bezalel miracles."

As Richard gazed down upon the city, the air felt electric. He hadn't been this happy since the night before the accident, and he thought about a day—hopefully not too far into the future—when he would get to share this experience with his family.

He turned to Rigot. "Thank you for making me do this."

"It's nothing, my friend. You helped make this happen. Without you, I'd still be in my apartment smashing old telephones and copiers to gather parts for a flying machine that wouldn't have worked. Now, with this balloon, I'm hopeful for the first time in centuries." Rigot reached out to shake Richard's hand.

Maybe it was the Bezalel spirit, or perhaps it was the desire for warmth, but in the moment, Richard grabbed Rigot's hand and pulled him closer for a friendly hug that lasted an awkwardly long time to the outside observer but was within the standards of comfort for Rigot.

"Bountiful Bezalel, my friend."

"Bountiful Bezalel," Richard repeated.

For the next hour, they traveled over the city and its snow-covered gardens, slowly ascending and discussing the lovely sights below.

"Look!" Richard shouted. "Hell of a Cup arranged their candles like an enormous coffee bean!"

"Nice," Rigot said. "I guess people always find a way to turn a sacred tradition into advertising."

Richard thought for a moment and laughed. "Hey! At least it isn't Democritus drinking out of a branded Hell of a Cup coffee mug!"

"Yes, my friend, at least they draw the line somewhere."

"Over there!" Richard pointed directly ahead. "They have candles set up around the trampoline in the shape of a giant sunflower!"

"Yes, my friend, they do that ev—" Rigot suddenly froze as if struck by a lightning bolt of fear. "Trampoline? The Great Projector!"

As they peered ahead into the darkness, Richard suddenly grasped what was alarming Rigot: they were on a direct collision course with the Great Projector! Its platform extended from a long metal arm protruding from the bottom of the incinerator door.

For those who zoned out during Aster's original explanation or who simply suffer from poor memory, the Great Projector was the name given to the piece of stagecraft magic Lucifer had built and installed near the incinerator door to create the illusion that Hell was still very much on fire for the benefit of the two large imbeciles responsible for tossing people into the incinerator.

"Hurry!" Rigot screamed. "We need to lower the balloon! The wind is taking us right into the projector!"

"How do we do that?"

"The valve! Open the air release valve on the balloon!" Rigot frantically searched for something.

"What valve?" Richard asked.

"The one hot air balloons have so they can release the hot air and descend rapidly!"

"You never said anything about a valve! Just a basket, a burner, and a balloon!"

"I thought you knew hot air balloons had valves! The balloon was your idea! Why would you propose a technology you know nothing about!"

With each passing second, they drew closer to the Great Projector.

"I'm sorry!" Richard shot back. "I'm just some guy who wasted his boring life! You're supposed to be the mad genius who knows everything about everything! The man who charmed Lucifer himself!"

The projector was now well within sight. The wind was picking up and accelerating their velocity.

Rigot stopped screaming for a moment to think. "I've got it! We just need to go up!" He opened the gas and lit the burner.

"But what if they open the door while we're up there? Those two big idiots could open it at any minute and see us."

"Yes, my friend, but if we destroy the projector, all of Hell will be found out. It's our only option. Lesser of two evils."

Richard nodded in agreement.

Rigot pulled on the gas valve without stopping, forcing the balloon higher, while Richard began untying ballasts to reduce the weight of the basket and accelerate their ascent.

As they approached the Great Projector, Richard could see they were going to pass over it with margin to spare. Better still, no one was opening the door as they passed nearby.

"We made it!" Rigot bellowed with relief.

"Woohoo!" Richard hollered in agreement.

They were less than a second from a celebratory embrace when they heard a loud *thud*, and the projector went dark.

Richard felt his heart stop, his stomach churn, and his rectum ascend into his throat.

Rigot peered over the edge of the basket, no doubt to catch a glimpse of the projector platform by the light of the burner before there was too much darkness between them to see anything. "Richard, my friend," he said in a tone that indicated he was trying to be calm while filled with rage, "when you were releasing the ballasts, did you make sure to fully untie all of them and watch each fall."

Richard, consumed by anxiety and shame, replied, "There was a lot going on. You were screaming. I was screaming. I'm not really sure."

"Oh," Rigot said through gritted teeth. "Okay, my friend. I only ask because when I look down there where the projector used to be, I see a smashed projector with a sandbag lying on top of it, and that sandbag sure looks a lot like one of our ballasts. So you can see why I'd think that."

Richard was distraught and without a word to defend himself. But it didn't matter. Before he could utter another word, there came a loud voice from the ground.

"You! Up there!" a man shouted through a megaphone that made his voice echo through the night air. "This is the Gehenna Guard. Please land the unauthorized aircraft now, or we will bring it down using force."

"Unauthorized aircraft?" Richard stared at Rigot. "I thought you said flying an aircraft was perfectly legal for recreational use!"

"It is, my friend, but like I said before, flying it to the incinerator door is illegal. Very, very, very, very, very . . . illegal."

Richard felt sick as the world seemed to spin around him. "Well, now what do we do?"

"We land, my friend. If not, they'll blow an enormous hole in our balloon and land it for us, and it'll hurt more than simply complying."

"Could we escape?" Richard asked, eager to avoid prison.

"In a balloon? No. Maybe if we had an actual flying machine, we'd have stood a chance. It's best if we land and explain it was a misunderstanding and hope for leniency. I'm an elected official, after all." Rigot signaled to the ground that he was going to comply by pointing to a clearing in the distance and shouting, "We're going to land! Don't shoot! Over there!"

A Bountiful Bezalel this turned out to be, Richard thought as they allowed the balloon to slowly descend.

Chapter 15
The Gestas

W ithout a release valve, it took a considerable time for
the balloon to land in the clearing. Coincidentally,
this also happened to be the same amount of time it took the
officers of the Gehenna Guard to become justifiably frustrated
by the whole ordeal and thus more aggressive than what would
have been considered reasonable.

As Rigot and Richard landed the balloon, they were met by
hundreds of guardsmen in yellow-and-green-striped uniforms
and bright-orange combat helmets that made it difficult to take
them seriously as any type of authority.

"My friends! The projector!" were the only words Rigot
could utter upon landing before he and Richard were yanked
from the basket, thrown to the ground, cuffed, and carted off to
the aptly named Gestas Detention and Rehabilitation Center
for People Who Did a Bad Thing but Who Aren't Necessarily
Bad People, or "The Gestas" for short.

The Gestas was one of the most glorious structures in all of
Gehenna. Its glass exterior gleamed with every color of the
rainbow, forming a large dome over an open area containing a

gargantuan lush garden with tables, beds, and lavatories spread throughout in a way that made it feel as though the inmates were living in a calm and soothing paradise—albeit, one without the slightest hint of privacy or personal space.

"This isn't what I expected when I envisioned us going to prison," Richard said, with delight, as he bounced on his bed. He took off his shirt and began changing into a gray inmate uniform.

"I know, my friend," Rigot replied. "It's truly terrible. A true Old Hell."

"What are you talking about?" Richard said. "This place is incredible! The beds are comfortable. The trees all have some nice-looking fruit, and the flowers and plants are gorgeous. Not to mention that the staff seems very friendly based on the conversation I had with the gentleman who booked us. Told me all about how his granddaughter plays some kind of ball-based sport for the Gehenna Guineas."

"Yes, my friend, but there's no privacy at all. No time to think, because there are people around all day and night checking in on you and making you take part in impromptu therapy sessions. You don't have the freedom to make an impact on the outside world when locked inside a glass dome. Life becomes a meaningless slog of self-improvement and inward reflection. Just you, fighting your demons in front of an audience."

Richard had a flashback to his time with Dr. Gregg and all at once understood what Rigot was saying. "Oh no. That *does* sound awful. Is there some shrink who makes you talk about your childhood and glue yarn to things?"

"Yes, my friend, hundreds of them. All day, every day, talking about your emotions, listening to others babble on about their rough lives as a vague justification for why they ended up here. It's relentless. And yarn. So much yarn. By the time we're free, you'll have glued enough yarn to make an entire wardrobe of itchy sweaters. And don't even get me started about the pipe cleaners."

"Wh-what about the inmates?" Richard asked, trembling with anxiety. "I remember Aster said some people aren't able to be rehabilitated. Truly awful people. Are they here? Are they a threat?"

"No. They aren't here. The truly awful people, like Genghis Khan, Adolf Hitler, and Vlad the Impaler, are kept in Soul Crush Cay, but don't let the name trip you up. It isn't what it sounds like."

"So," Richard said, confused, "it isn't soul crushing?"

"Oh, it's absolutely soul crushing," Rigot explained, "but it isn't actually a cay. It's more of an atoll. Truly awful people can't be a part of our society. We've found the best use for them is administration."

"Administration? Like running things?"

"No. That'd be absurd, my friend. All of these people—what they have in common is a love of power. Even your average serial killer often suffers from a complex where murder makes him feel powerful and motivates him. Therefore, Soul Crush Cay starts by giving them meaningless office work. This could be approving forms or signing off on permits and requisitions—something bureaucratic and truly pointless in its significance—but it gives them a small amount of power. It's just enough that it constantly reminds them of the power they crave—but not enough to truly satisfy the craving. It's like being thirsty but only receiving a single drop of water on your tongue each day as a reminder of how satisfying it would be to quench your thirst. It crushes their souls and causes their own cravings to drive them mad."

"So they torment themselves?" Richard clarified.

"Who better to do the job, my friend? They're experts at

causing pain and misery. The only difference between your well-known sociopath and your average mid-level bureaucrat or homeowners' association president is scale. One uses a lot of power to cause a lot of pain to his fellow human, while the other uses a small amount of power to cause a lot of pain to his fellow human. I'd argue the ounce of pain produced per ounce of power is more efficient with the bureaucrats and association presidents, but that's not the scale of misery that gets you in the history books. Taking that lust for power and reducing the scale to near inconsequentiality has proven to be the best way to crush their souls."

Before Richard could ask his next question, a giant—eight feet tall, give or take—stepped from behind a nearby line of citrus trees, locked eyes on him, and darted in his direction. The giant was made of solid muscle and had shoulder-length, wavy red hair and a chiseled face covered in battle scars. He looked like a relic from a more brutal period in human history— an old soul who smelled of old soles and old sole.

Richard didn't know this giant, but he anticipated an immense amount of physical discomfort in his near future.

"This is my bed," the giant groaned, pointing to Richard.

"I-I-I-I'm very sorry," Richard said, shaking with fear as he stood to make way. "This is where they told me to sleep."

"Is that so?" asked the giant, without a hint of emotion in his voice.

"Yes, it's so," Rigot interjected in his defense.

The giant's face softened, and he offered a delightfully friendly smirk. "Then it is okay. I can sleep elsewhere. It is not a big deal."

He's doing that thing where he pretends it's okay but then tries to kill me in my sleep, thought Richard, unsure whether the giant was sincere or sarcastic.

"I know I look scary," the giant said. "I get that a lot. I am kind. Do not judge me by my appearance."

"Of course, my friend," Rigot replied. "We'd never dream of such a thing. Looking at you, I'm guessing you were a warrior. Likely a great and mighty one at that!"

"Yes. I was a warrior in the Walrus Wars," the giant replied. "Not a good one. I was a big target. I did not last long." The giant chuckled at his own misfortune, fully relieving the remaining tension in the air.

"Well, it's nice to meet you, my friend," Rigot replied. "I'm Rigot, and this is Richard. This is our first night here, so we're still getting the lay of the land."

"Welcome," the giant replied. "My name is Parataxis."

"Parataxis! Now that, my friend, is a mighty warrior's name if I've ever heard one!" Rigot exclaimed, in a transparent attempt to flatter the giant. "You sure it wasn't Parataxis the Potent or Parataxis the Powerful?"

"No," Parataxis replied, with a bashful grin. "I was not a potent warrior. I was not a powerful warrior. I was just a large warrior. I was just a prodigious Parataxis."

"Well, my friend, I am going to call you Parataxis the Pleasant because you seem like such a nice fellow."

"I approve," Parataxis said. "I write poetry. I like Parataxis the Poet. You can call me that."

"Ooh, I like that too!" Rigot shouted, with delight. "Parataxis the Prodigious Pleasant Poet! You'll have to perform some of your poetry periodically! I presume it's pretty! Poetically pulchritudinous and perfectly pleasing, perchance?"

Parataxis's face lit up with amusement, but the thrill was short-lived.

A squat, stubby woman in white scrubs suddenly appeared as if from nowhere and injected herself into the conversation. "Hiii! I'm Meredith!" she said, with an air of faux friendliness and artificial enthusiasm. She wore her brown hair in a tight bun atop her head, and her matching bright-red glasses and lipstick reminded Richard of his fourth-grade choir teacher. "I'll be your facilitator tonight! I'm here to observe and provide guidance, but don't let me interrupt. Just pretend like I'm not here." She smiled an unconvincing smile and then held her clipboard to her chest in preparation for taking notes.

Richard exchanged glances with Rigot and Parataxis, looked at Meredith, and then glanced at the other men again. How were they supposed to continue with someone monitoring their conversation? "So," he said in an attempt to break the awkward silence, "poetry, you say."

"Yes," Parataxis replied. "Poetry."

"Richard," Meredith said, "tell me about your father."

The question caught Richard off guard. "Excuse me?"

"Tell me about your father," Meredith repeated. "There are no judgments here. Was your father ashamed of you? Is that what led you to a life of crime?"

"Are we really doing this right now?" Richard muttered to Meredith. "In front of everyone? Don't you have some kind of facilitator-patient confidentiality?"

Meredith smiled. "Confidentiality? We're all friends here! It's important we be open with those around us on our rehabilitation journey."

What do I need to do to get transferred to Soul Crush Cay? Richard wondered, staving off another panic attack.

"Did your father tell you that you weren't enough?" Meredith continued. "Do you feel like he was too lenient on you, and that's why you make poor decisions? Was he—"

"Excuse me," Rigot said. "Meredith, is it?"

"Don't interrupt," Meredith snapped, oblivious to the hypocrisy. "It's rude."

"Yes, I understand that," Rigot replied. "But, you see,

tonight when we were on the balloon ride that landed us here, we accidentally damaged the visual apparatus of the Great Projector. It still produces heat and sound, but the images of the flames of Old Hell are no longer functioning. Fortunately, it'll be mostly dark for several weeks, so it's possible no one will notice unless they intentionally look down, but someone has to go up there and repair the projector before we have an extended period of daylight, or someone will surely realize that Hell is no longer on fire."

Meredith took notes on her clipboard without looking up. "So you two irresponsibly took a balloon to the incinerator door and destroyed the projector, dooming us all? Is that right?"

"Yes, I'm afraid that's true," a remorseful Richard answered.

"And do you think you did this because you two suffer from substance abuse problems?" asked Meredith, exuding the warmth of a speculum. "Maybe cocaine or opioids? People who do irrational and impulsive things like fly a balloon to the incinerator door on Bezalel and destroy property are either under the influence of narcotics or unbelievably stupid. Would you like to talk about that? Maybe I can help you find the root cause of your addiction."

"Madam!" Rigot yelled. "I assure you, neither of us does any type of illicit substances. But if someone doesn't get up there soon and fix the projector, we're all in big trouble!"

Meredith stood silently for a moment as if pausing to process Rigot's words. "Well, it sounds like the first thing we need to do is discuss your denial. Being honest with ourselves about our addiction is the first step to recovery."

I barely know this woman, Richard thought as Rigot continued to try to explain the severity of the situation, *and I already hate her.*

Chapter 16
Then All Hell Broke Loose

Warrior dad fierce, not wise,
Tried to fish, caught his eyes.
Warrior stance, tripped on logs,
Battle cries silenced by dogs.
Longship built, sailed so free,
Backward oars, lost at sea.
Forged a sword, handle too short,
Fumbled fights, lost our fort.
Teaching son to raid with might,
Overslept, missed the fight.
Wore horned helmet to impress,
Stuck in doorways, caused distress.
Warrior dad, blunders told,
Love and laughter, stories unfold.
A dad of yore, flawed but bold,
Fondness and folly in sagas retold.
—Parataxis the Poet

As Parataxis read his latest poem aloud at the weekly Puppies & Poetry therapy session at the Gestas, Richard listened attentively alongside Rigot and a dozen or so fellow inmates seated in a semicircle. In these mutually beneficial gatherings, the inmates expressed their emotions creatively while comforted by newborn canines, and the puppies learned an early lesson in human cruelty by being subjected to hours of amateur poetry.

It was better than yarn art, Richard told himself.

"That was . . . *interesting*," Meredith said afterward. "How does it make you feel to talk about your father? Do you feel shame when you talk about his failings? Do you feel his weaknesses reflect upon your own character? Perhaps that being an incompetent failure is genetic, and that's why you're here to begin with?"

"I am no failure," Parataxis replied, thrusting out his chest in righteous indignation. "I was a victim of my genetics. Born large, not incompetent. Not my fault. How could I have known walrus were such skillful warriors?"

"Well, those sound like the words of a man unwilling to take ownership of his character flaws," Meredith said, with an unsettling smirk, before scribbling something on her clipboard. For someone who loved to use the phrase, "There are no judgments here," she seemed to relish passing judgment on her patients at every possible opportunity.

Meredith's tactless nature was more than Richard could bear. He found her presence grating—so much so that he inadvertently petted his dachshund puppy, Mr. Wienerbottom, a bit too hard, causing the poor animal to yelp in pain.

"Mr. Wilkins!" Meredith shouted, turning to Richard. "Get your comfort puppy under control!"

Richard scrambled to make amends with Mr. Wienerbottom, gently petting him and scratching behind his ears. Richard had been in the Gestas for all of five days and already found himself pushed to the edge of sanity by Meredith and her continuous backhanded compliments, ridicule, insulting questions, and forced smile that masked her intended malice. The mere sound of her voice caused his left eye to twitch and his right hand to begin rubbing his thigh in long strokes without him noticing.

Rigot, on the other hand, seemed to be having a splendid time with his new friend, a bulldog named Sire Snortington. "Who's my slobbery baby?" he whispered to the noble heir to the Snortington throne, oblivious to everyone else in the room. "*You* are. *You* are."

Meredith pointed to Richard while addressing the group. "You see, this is why you shouldn't do drugs. Next thing you know you'll be hurting defenseless animals for kicks!"

"I'm sorry." Richard seethed, teeth clenched, finally having had enough. "What are your qualifications to treat patients? Are you a licensed rehabilitation professional? Did you go to school for this?"

"That's quite enough, Mr. Wilkins!" Meredith replied. "I'll have you know I attended days of training prior to starting this position."

"*Days?*" he shouted, incredulous. Standing up to an authority for the first time in his life sent his heart racing and shock waves through his entire body. "Not years. Not months. Not weeks. Just *days?* And that somehow qualifies you to accuse me and my friend of being drug addicts or idiots? It qualifies you to tell poor Parataxis that his death in battle is a personal failing?"

"Mr. Wilkins!" Meredith frantically shouted. "I said, that's quite enough!"

"Oh, no. No, no, no. It's not enough. Not even close!"

Richard was growing angrier by the moment. "My whole life—shit, my whole *death*—I just did what I felt I had to do to get to the next thing and make others happy. I took a job in a factory to care for my wife. I took a promotion I really didn't want to provide a better living for my family and make my boss happy, which ended up getting me killed! Hell! I went up in the balloon with Rigot because I thought it would make *him* happy! Not once did I ever think about what *I* wanted, what would make *me* happy! But I'm done letting the universe drag me from point to point without consideration for what I want. I'm done with letting it boss me around. And I'm done letting you bully and insult me!"

Meredith tried to interject.

But Richard pointed an accusing finger at her. "You humiliate us. You belittle us. And you do it with a smile on your face. You think that smile makes it okay? All of the things you could have chosen eternity to do, and you chose to spend it tormenting others under the guise of treatment! You're a red-lipped monster! You're the first person I've met in Hell who actually deserves to be sent to Hell, and not the nice one; the shitty old one that was all flames and torment!"

Richard finally stopped screaming when he noticed a strange, swirling mixture of relief and dread. His heart still raced, and his arms tingled with pins and needles.

The room fell silent. A puppy whimpered.

Richard prepared for Meredith to have him punished for his outburst.

"Mr. Wilkins," she said in a surprisingly reserved tone. "You're free to go. Please take this note to the agent at the door and collect your things."

"Excuse me?" Richard said, confused.

"You're free to go," Meredith repeated to him, with her first sincere smile since his arrival. "Rehabilitation is about getting to the source of our problems and addressing them in a real and meaningful way, which you just did. You said it yourself: you spent your whole life just going where the wind took you, avoiding conflict and making others happy, not thinking about what you wanted or having the courage to stand up and demand what would make you happy. That behavior is what killed you. That's what got you here. Your desire to be liked and to please others at the cost of your own happiness has led to so much pain, like tarts and teapots. But you recognized that behavior, and you took action to change it. You broke loose from it, and now you're free to go."

Richard was lost in thought as he placed Mr. Wienerbottom in Meredith's arms.

She gave him a slip of paper and a wink that indicated she knew more than she had let on.

"Thank you," he said, still not fully understanding what had just happened. "I think."

A loud commotion followed, and Richard turned to see Rigot standing behind his seat, holding Sire Snortington in one arm and slapping the back of his chair with the other.

"Meredith!" Rigot squinted, as he made an unconvincing angry face while shaking a finger at her. "You're a bitch, and I hate you! I hope Lucifer returns so he can reignite a small patch of Hell just for you! Your red glasses make you look like an art teacher! And not in a good way!"

Meredith rolled her eyes in frustration. "Sit down. That's not gonna work. You can't just insult me and hope to be released. You have to work out your own issues."

"Oh, I'm sorry," Rigot said, calmly taking a seat. "I take back what I said about your glasses. They're actually quite lovely and frame your eyes nicely." He smiled nervously.

Richard felt bad for leaving Rigot and gave him a guilt-ridden frown.

Rigot returned Richard's gaze with a nod that indicated he understood. It was time for Richard to go.

Richard made his way through the Gestas's gardens on his way to the exit. He thought about what had just transpired and the lesson he was supposed to take from his experience.

I yelled. I was combative. And it felt good.

Great, actually.

The world didn't end. I shouldn't fear conflict and the judgment of others.

Richard noticed a sudden spring in his step and an overwhelming sense of joy he hadn't felt in decades—like a burden had been lifted from his shoulders. He felt as if he had spent his entire existence as a clenched fist, and for the first time, he was free to be open.

I can't let myself be controlled by trying to make others happy. I have to advocate for my own happiness. I'm in control of my destiny. I—

His thoughts were interrupted by the sound of millions of people screaming all at once outside the glass dome of the Gestas. He glanced around, trying to find the source of the screaming.

A loud *crash* shook the dome, and rainbow-colored glass rained down from above.

Richard ducked and covered his eyes to avoid the falling shards.

The screams grew louder.

Flames erupted within the gardens, smoke filled the gardens, and he was enveloped in darkness, unable to see more than a foot in front of his face.

Inmates raced past him screeching in pain and panic, shoving and knocking him down.

Everything transpired within seconds—so fast Richard couldn't be sure it was really happening.

"Rigot!" he shouted, as he struggled to stand amid the stampede, flames growing closer by the second.

Chapter 17
Then All Heaven Broke Loose

"Rigot!" Richard shouted as he fought to stand.

He placed a hand on the ground to try to push himself up, only to experience a sudden rush of pain as his nose crashed into the knee of an unseen inmate in the never-ending stampede. The contact knocked him back to the ground in agony without slowing the stampede in the slightest.

The fire grew closer, but Richard was blinded by the pain of being continuously trampled and kicked by the onslaught of fleeing inmates.

A second later, he was levitating through the smoke and darkness at an astounding rate of speed. The sensation felt oddly familiar, like something from a long-forgotten memory, but he couldn't recollect ever having the ability to levitate and figured if he had such an ability, he'd surely remember. Then it occurred to him that he was being held in an enormous pair of arms like a sleeping child carried to bed by a parent.

Rigot's voice pierced the darkness. "It's okay. We have you, my friend,"

"Is that you, Rigot?" Richard asked, befuddled by Rigot's newfound physical strength.

"Yes, it's me, my friend. The Gestas is ablaze! We must find a way out!"

"How are you doing this, Rigot?" Richard mumbled, still dazed from the impact and unable to see through the smoke.

"I'm not sure what you mean. But now isn't the time for chatting, my friend."

Richard agreed. He continued to exist in a delicate state of balance between consciousness and unconsciousness, trying to stay awake. He passed out before regaining a few seconds of awareness—long enough to see the smoke and flames moving past him in the darkness.

The air suddenly became frigid. The screaming of millions became more unbearable. Richard sensed they were outside. He fought to open his eyes for just a second and saw snow, ash, and balls of flame falling from the dark sky.

"What's happening?" he muttered, barely able to move his lips.

"I think someone realized Hell was no longer Hell much quicker than we'd hoped," Rigot replied.

As they traveled under the light of a lamppost, Richard used his remaining strength to force his eyes open for an extended period. He saw Parataxis's face and a set of arms wrapped around his neck. The arms belonged to Rigot, who was attached to Parataxis's back like a human backpack, his head resting on the giant's broad shoulders.

"Parataxis," Richard said, as he lost the battle for consciousness.

———

W hen Richard came to, he found himself lying on a damp rock. His back and neck ached, and his head throbbed with pain. He looked around and saw that he lay next to a small fire in a stone cavern. The sullen faces of Rigot and Parataxis glowed in the firelight.

"Where are we?" Richard stared up at the cave ceiling and applied pressure to his pounding forehead.

"In the caverns below Mount Molay, my friend," Rigot answered.

"Why? What happened?"

"They burned it all," Parataxis said.

"All?"

"Yes, my friend, all," Rigot answered in a devastated voice. "They burned the entire city of Gehenna. The gardens. The Biblio. The museums. The apartments. All of it. Gone. Hell is once again ablaze."

"How is that possible?"

"It seems as though they'd planned for this, my friend. Like the reigniting of Hell was something in GOD's corporate contingency plans. Millions of angels and souls descended upon the city with incendiary devices. They set up some type of machine on the old projector platform to launch giant flaming meteors. Before anyone could even mount a response, everything we built, everything we worked so hard for over millennia was gone. Just ash floating in the wind."

Parataxis shook his head at the shame of it all.

"Is there anything we can do?" Richard asked, desperately trying to find the light in all this darkness.

"No, my friend. Now that they know, they won't stop until they reignite every inch of Hell. Having this place as a tool to keep people under control is too valuable an asset to the company. I'm sure they'll keep staff here to monitor and ensure we can never find comfort again. All hope is truly lost."

For the first time, Rigot didn't seem to be himself. He wasn't confident. He wasn't unashamed. Quite the opposite, he seemed hopeless and riddled with guilt for his part in bringing about Hell's destruction.

Fortunately, Richard also didn't feel like himself. Perhaps it was the revelation with Meredith. Perhaps it was brain damage from the trampling. But he sat up and locked eyes with Rigot. "So that's it? We give up?"

"Yes," Rigot answered. "There's no way. Lucifer is gone, Hell is ablaze, and GOD is now in full control. I've thought of every possible outcome, and short of a miracle, there's no way for things to go back to what they were yesterday."

Richard sat silent for a moment, hand on his chin, deep in thought. "Rigot, did you arrive in Hell before or after the Bezalel Brotherhood put out the flames of Hell?"

"When I arrived, they were mostly done. Only some far-flung areas were still ablaze. But they were so far from the city, I never got a chance to see them. I don't see how that's relevant, though. We can't repeat what they did under GOD's watchful eye."

"Yes," Richard replied, "I know that, but can you imagine what they thought the odds were of being able to fix all of Hell?"

"You're oversimplifying, my friend," Rigot replied. "I know you want to have hope. People get addicted to hope, but hope has no basis in reality. You can't hope Hell back into being what it was. I have thought through every scenario, and there are none where we can fix this."

"That isn't my point." Richard stood up and began pacing. "They didn't set out to fix all of Hell, right? They were just trying to create an oasis at the beginning. One small thing.

Then another small thing. They never thought about the insurmountable odds of fixing Hell but just did the next thing they could, then the next one, and then the next, and one day, they'd changed all of Hell. We don't need a master plan. We don't need the odds. We just need to think about what the next best step is and do that."

Rigot chuckled, shaking his head in disbelief. "Richard, doing the 'next best thing' without a plan is what you told Meredith was the cause of your mediocre life and death. Something about being blown in the wind. You always did the next thing in front of you with no plan. Now it's the solution to all our problems?"

"Yes." Richard felt surprisingly chipper for a man who had just doomed an entire dimension. "My problem wasn't that I always did the next best thing. It was that I did them without asking myself if they were the next best thing toward some greater good rather than the path of least resistance. I took the path with the least immediate pain, not the best one. We need to decide what we want to achieve. Then we take the first step, then the next. It may not be easy, but we must endure the pain, and maybe one day we can fix things. We have eternity, after all."

"Are you okay, my friend?" Rigot asked.

"I've never been better!" Richard exclaimed. "So here are the first steps. The way I see it, we should start by exploring these caves to see if we can rebuild here. Maybe the new Hell is underground. Maybe it isn't bringing back what we once had but finding a new path to escape the flames."

Rigot leapt to his feet in astonishment. "Richard! You stupid . . . brilliant . . . idiot! That's it! We can't build what we had because GOD will expect it, but we can do something new. A new Hell that they'd never expect. No one even knows these caverns are here. I only know because Lucifer once brought me here, and he's long gone, so I'm the only person who knows they exist. We could expand them and bring in more souls to help, and it could grow exponentially as we brought in more souls, just like the extinguishing of the flames."

The next thing he knew, Richard found himself being wrapped in Rigot's arms as Rigot gave him the longest, most awkward embrace of their relationship, which was quite an accomplishment, Richard thought, given their history.

Rigot overflowed with enthusiasm. "I love you, my friend!"

Richard, for the first time, felt as though he understood his purpose, and his heart began to swell with pride.

Parataxis stood up and joined the embrace, lifting Richard and Rigot in his arms. "I love you guys as well."

All hugging out of the way, Richard, Rigot, and Parataxis sat around the fire.

Rigot picked up a small chip of stone and began to etch into the rocky floor of the cave a map of the caverns. "Okay, my friends, so this way leads to Lucifer's Point, and if we go this way, it's a bit longer but leads to Lucifer's Gulch. Over here is a small cut, Lucifer's Cut."

"Is everything here named for Lucifer?" Richard asked.

"Of course not!" Rigot replied. "The tightest cavern is Joe's Asshole, for obvious reasons."

Richard glanced at a blank-faced Parataxis and then at Rigot, without changing his expression.

"Get it?" Rigot asked. "Because he's a tight-ass? Tightest cavern? Joe's Asshole?" He laughed to himself, clearly more amused by the joke than Richard or Parataxis. "Well, I thought it was a good name. So. Joe's Asshole." Rigot pointed to the passage on his sketched map. "I think that's where we should start. It's the hardest to get through, so if we could make a passage and expand an opening farther down, it would likely be too narrow for unwanted visitors to willingly wander into in the future."

Richard and Parataxis nodded in agreement.

"Lead the way," Richard said with a smirk, pointing an open palm in the direction of Joe's Asshole.

Rigot lit a makeshift torch from the flame of the campfire and did just that.

As they approached Joe's Asshole, they found it was indeed very tight. Richard and Rigot barely squeezed inside Joe's Asshole, while Parataxis was too big to fit.

"Wait there!" Rigot shouted back to Parataxis. "We'll just get a quick look inside and come back."

"So I was thinking," Richard said, as they made their way through the passage. "If we end up using this place, we're going to rename this cavern, right?"

"Why would we do that, my friend? Lucifer named these caverns. The names have sentimental value."

"Ah, of course, of course," Richard replied, trying his best to be tactful. "But what if we just called it JA?"

"No." Rigot gave Richard a stern look. "It was one of Lucifer's better jokes. He was pretty proud of it. Get used to it. Besides, I'm sure after a few millennia, people will cram it all together and call it something like Josasole anyway. Like what they did in Idaho."

"Idaho?" Richard stepped on a pile of rocks that immediately gave way, sending him careening down a dark and icy tunnel.

Rigot's voice trailed after him. "Richard!"

The tunnel descended at an angle such that Richard could slide down it but not stop his descent. "Shit! Shit! Shit! Shit! Shit!" he repeated dozens of times as he fell down the dark tunnel with no light.

"I'm right behind you!" came Rigot's voice.

They both landed in a small cavity, no larger than an average walk-in closet and barely tall enough for the average person to stand inside.

As Richard landed, he heard a loud click, as if the cavity floor had shifted just slightly on impact, and then the sound of a ticking clock.

"Are you okay?" Rigot asked, hunched over in the small cavity.

"Yes, I'm fine. My butt's a little sore, but I'm fine." Richard was still trying to find his bearings.

Rigot held the torch to the wall as if something had caught his eye in the flicker of the flame. The walls were covered in small cavities a few inches wide, and each had a shaped stone within it, fit snuggly like a puzzle piece. The stones had been carved into the shapes of hammers, nails, trees, seas, scythes, flies, spoons, forks, bowls and rings, ships with sails, cabbages, and kings, among many, many other things. In the middle of it all were the words, written in all caps and reddish brown and splotchy, as if scrawled in blood, *TEAPOTS RIGOT*.

Rigot smacked his forehead and began jumping up and down, unable to control his excitement. He turned to Richard. "It's Lucifer. He's here."

Chapter 18
When Life Gives You Lemons

"What do you think this means?" Richard asked, examining the wall of shaped stones and their matching compartments.

"It's a puzzle," Rigot answered. "I imagine wherever Lucifer is, he doesn't want others to find him, but he left me a path as his closest friend. Knowing the way he thinks, I imagine removing the wrong piece will trap us in here forever, and picking the correct one will somehow lead us closer to him. I'm assuming we activated some kind of timer on impact, and now there's a clock ticking down for us to choose. He always loved a good puzzle and had a gift for engineering."

The ticking seemed to grow louder.

Richard continued to analyze the wall, looking for something but not sure what. "Aha!" he exclaimed. "I found it! The tart! It's that silly thing people here in Hell keep saying: 'tarts and teapots,' right?" He reached for the stone tart.

"Stop!" Rigot knocked Richard's hand aside. "Just stop! You don't know anything about anything."

"Hey!" Richard shouted. "What else could it possibly be? That 'tarts and teapots' thing is like some secret code only demons and government officials seem to know. Aster said it. Meredith said it. That must be it."

"No, my friend," Rigot said, in a tone that suggested he was growing frustrated with Richard's confidence. "First of all, that phrase was something he commonly said. He said it all the time. Anyone who met him likely heard him say it. Others probably heard it from those who heard it from Lucifer and passed it on. So it isn't some secret phrase that he'd use as a code. Second, that stone is a pie, not a tart. It has an upper crust etched on it. Apparently, you don't know a damned thing about Lucifer, *or* pastries, for that matter."

"Oh," Richard replied. "Well, do you know which stone to pick?"

"No, my friend, I don't. But I imagine that's the idea. There's something in the story of the phrase that he told me that only I know as probably the only person he shared it with. We just need to think about the details of the story to find the answer."

"You're about to make me listen to a story in this tiny, dark cavern, aren't you?" Richard asked, suddenly feeling anxious. "We don't even know how much time we have."

"Yes, my friend, but I'll try to make it quick. The phrase is more than just a catchy alliteration. It's an affirmation. Do you remember when I told you that Lucifer had everything as a child but always wanted more?"

"Yes, of course," Richard replied. "It was one of the first stories you told me about him."

"Well, when he was an adolescent, one of their servants surprised him with a lemon tart. He hadn't had one before and very much enjoyed it. She was delighted at his enjoyment. But rather than be thankful to the servant, he immediately demanded another. Unfortunately, they were out of lemons, and his mother, being a compassionate person, refused to force the servant to go purchase more so close to the end of her workday. Thus, Lucifer became even more upset, and in his obsession with wanting more, he let himself into the kitchen and began rummaging through the cabinets to see if he could make one himself. He just wouldn't be happy with the joy of the first one. He needed *more*. In his rummaging, he carelessly knocked a teapot out of the serving cabinet, shattering it. But it wasn't just any teapot. This teapot was priceless to his mother. It had been passed down from her grandfather Russell, and was the only heirloom she had from a grandfather she loved very much. She was distraught. Didn't speak for weeks. She tried to have it repaired, but it was never the same, and whenever she looked at it, she just felt more sadness."

"That's horrible," Richard said. "Lucifer must've felt terrible."

"He did, my friend. Lucifer could be selfish, discontent, and moody, but he was always kind and never meant to hurt his mother. That mistake stuck with him for the rest of his life, and whenever he'd start to feel obsession or discontent, he'd say, 'It's tarts and teapots!' to remind himself that focusing on the desire for the things he didn't have, rather than being content with what he *did* have, would only lead to pain. Sure, he couldn't always live up to the message of his mantra, but it helped."

Richard sat on the hard floor of the cavern for a moment, disassembling the elements of the story. "Lemons!" he shouted. "I bet the answer is lemons!"

They began examining every stone in the cavity wall in search of a lemon but found nothing of the sort.

"Okay," Richard said, "maybe not lemons, but what else could it be? Maybe a dustpan to represent the servant?"

They searched the wall but found no dustpan or other cleaning implement.

"The fork!" Richard yelled. "Did he mention if he ate it with a fork?"

"No, I don't remember the utensils being mentioned in the story."

"But that must be it, right? What else could it be at this point? Perhaps you just forgot after all this time."

Rigot didn't answer and instead stared blankly at the puzzle wall, apparently lost in thought.

The ticking was causing Richard to become more anxious by the minute. If it stopped, he worried, they'd be trapped in the cavity for eternity. "I'm going with the fork," he said, reaching for the stone in the shape of a fork. "It's our best bet."

Rigot suddenly broke from his trance and leapt toward him, tackling him to the ground before he could reach for the fork stone. "I have it, my friend!" Rigot said, while lifting himself off Richard. "The answer is none! *'TEAPOTS RIGOT'* isn't 'Your clue is teapots, Rigot.' It's 'Always remember, tarts and teapots, Rigot.' Lucifer knew me as well as I knew him. He knew I'd be discontent with the time we shared before he left and would become obsessed with finding him, and he knew that obsession would cause me pain. The answer isn't anything on this wall. The answer is to stop trying to find him. Let the clock run out."

"That's insane!" Richard howled. "Why build this giant puzzle if none is the answer? You're going to get us trapped in this damned cavity with your philosophical bullshit!"

"No, my friend! You had to know the man like I did. It's chaos! It makes sense because it doesn't make sense! Please! Just trust me." Rigot's eyes, lit by the light of the flickering torch, begged for Richard's trust.

"Okay," Richard said, "I'm going to trust you, but I swear, if this doesn't work and we end up trapped in this cave forever,

I'll spend every waking moment reminding you what an idiot you are."

"That's fair, my friend," Rigot replied.

They stood side by side, waiting for the ticking to end.

Then it did.

Just as the ticking stopped, a large stone fell from the ceiling, covering the tunnel opening and trapping them inside.

"I told you!" Richard shouted. "Now we're trapped!"

"Hold on." Rigot, turning to hold the torch up to the stone, illuminated a single compartment, which contained a small button in the shape of a lemon. "Well, my friend, I guess you were right. It was the lemon after all." He smiled at Richard. "Would you like to do the honors?"

Richard dashed over to the stone and pushed the button as quickly as possible, eager to escape the cavity. A loud *crack* followed, and the wall behind them split open, spitting rocks and dust and revealing the other half of the cavity, a table, and a passageway.

Parataxis's voice echoed from the other side of the passage. "Roses are red. Violets are blue. I am Parataxis. How are you?"

"Probably his best poem yet," Rigot joked. "Parataxis the Prolific Pleasant Poet!"

As they approached the table, two boxes on the tabletop came into the light of their torch. They were square but shallow and were of the same relative dimensions as a large pizza delivery box. One was made with an aged off-white plastic and had a black screen containing green text on the top and a gray mechanical keyboard implanted in the area of the cover below the screen. The other, stainless steel and sleek, featured a holographic screen and a flush keyboard that lit the bottom of the cover. One looked cheap, outdated, and obsolete, while the other looked like it cost a fortune.

Richard found himself naturally more drawn to the sleek and expensive device.

Apparently, Rigot felt the same way. He placed his hand within an inch of the keyboard, and the screen lit up with the hologram of an exploding supernova.

A feminine robotic voice emanated from the speaker on the side of the box: "Welcome to Aesthetic Observable Dimension. Please enter your password to continue."

Rigot pulled back his hand and glanced at Richard with an expression of shock. "This . . . This . . . This is AOD! It must be Lucifer's first observable dimension kit!"

"That's amazing!" Richard shouted. "You think he's in there? Do you know the password?"

Rigot paused for a moment. "No, my friend, I don't know his password, but I could give it a guess. Lucile was his mother's name. Let's try that." He typed the word and pushed *enter*.

The box chimed loudly. "I'm sorry, that password is incorrect. You can try again in one minute."

"Try lemons," Richard suggested. "It worked last time."

They waited a minute and entered the next guess.

"I'm sorry," the box responded. "That password is incorrect. You can try again in five minutes."

Richard and Rigot spent the next five minutes debating the best password and settled on Russell's Teapot, both due to its meaningfulness and its secure verbosity.

Rigot entered the two words.

"I'm sorry," the box responded. "That password is incorrect. You can try again in ten thousand years."

"Ten thousand years!" Richard exclaimed. "That's a hell of a jump from five minutes!"

"Important things require strict security I guess." Rigot strained to hide the disappointment in his voice. "Well, it seems we'll have some time to wait. Why don't we take these two boxes and make our way down the passage back to Parataxis."

Rigot picked up the AOD box and placed it under his arm, Richard picked up the old junk box and carried it on his outstretched arm like a pizza delivery driver, and they headed down the passage to meet up with a waiting Parataxis.

"We heard your poem," Rigot said, as they approached Parataxis at the campsite. "We're fine. How are you?"

"I am well," Parataxis replied, missing the allusion to his poem.

Richard placed the junk box at his feet and sat in front of the campfire. He noticed the screen had gone black and was concerned he had perhaps broken it during transport. He pressed the space bar.

The screen lit up in the form of a bespectacled man's face made of green text. "Hey!" the box said, in a voice that was reminiscent of an elderly English gentleman's. "Try poking yourself down there and see how you feel about it!"

"Excuse me?" Richard said, startled by the response.

"Oh, it's quite all right," the box said. "I've just been sitting on that bloody table for the past few millennia, and my first human contact is someone poking me right in the space bar. It's startling and a bit forward, you know? Next time, you can buy me a drink before getting all handsy."

Rigot set his AOD box on the ground and joined Richard. "Sorry for my friend's groping and poking," he said, glancing at Richard with a smirk.

Richard was both embarrassed and confused by his apparent faux pas. He paused to contemplate the various levels of implied intimacy of keyboard keys, which only made his choice of space bar all the more humiliating.

"Oh, it's really not a problem," the box said, in a kind and reassuring tone. "Better than sitting on that table with that other box that blabbers on about passwords century after century."

"Very good then," Rigot said. "I'm Rigot, and these are my friends, Richard and Parataxis."

"It's nice to make your acquaintances," the box replied. "I'm Observable Dimension One, but people call me One for short."

"One!" Rigot howled with excitement. "I know all about you! You're Joe's first observable dimension!"

"Oh, knock it off with the flattery," One said. "No one cares about an old observable dimension kit with the most mundane simulation imaginable."

Richard suppressed a laugh. It was obvious the older box with no password was insecure and hoping for more compliments. "Of course we care," he said. "Joe went on to create the dimension we came from." He glanced at Rigot and then Parataxis, attempting to gauge their sentiment on the matter.

"Is that so?" One asked, clearly trying to extract more kind words. "From the conversations I have had with his old business partner, I assumed that the fellow would be incapable of creating anything with life forms as sentient as yourselves."

"Lucifer!" Rigot shouted, incapable of holding back his delight. "We tried some passwords on the AOD box so we could try to find Lucifer in there, but we ended up locking ourselves out. You wouldn't happen to know the password, would you?"

The pride in One's voice indicated he was very much enjoying being the center of attention. "Yes, I do. It's just 'password1234.'"

That's my password too, Richard thought. *Don't know why I didn't try it first.*

"Well, we're locked out from trying again for ten thousand years," Rigot said. "Know any way around that?"

"No, I'm sorry," One answered. "Trying would be a waste of time anyway."

"I understand," Rigot said, with a look of defeat. "It's clearly a very advanced box."

"Oh, no, that's not it," One said, pausing for dramatic effect. "It's a waste because he isn't in there. He's in me."

Chapter 19
We All Make Mistakes

The contemplation of time is generally a waste of time—that is, if something infinite can even be wasted.

Before we can discuss time, we first must establish a common framework for its measurement. Humans have largely created these measurements based on the orbit of the home planet around its star, the rotation of the home planet on its axis, and the orbit of its moon, since those are generally constant. It certainly doesn't hurt that if they stopped being constant measures, their critics would likely be too preoccupied with surviving the subsequent apocalypse to gloat about it.

For the sake of common understanding, let's use the concept of the relative Earth year, month, and day as our basis for the discussion of time. This would make the most sense, since the planet Earth spins at relatively the same speed each day and orbits its sun at generally the same speed each year—and because twelve staggered fluctuations of thirty and thirty-one axis rotations with a single twenty-eight rotation month that is twenty-nine rotations every four times the Earth orbits

its sun is unarguably the best and easiest way to understand measure of time in any reality.

Time is also relative to the observer. For example, time on Earth runs at two times the relative speed of the Heaven and Hell dimensions—the benefit of this being that the simulation runs faster than the parent dimension that observes it, thus reaching conclusions first, making the data generated highly valuable from a predictive standpoint. However, to an observer on Earth, time would seem to be moving slowly in the Heaven dimension by a factor of two, which is why time often seems to slow down during a near-death experience or when watching the clock at work while your soul slowly dies . . .

————

"How long has Lucifer been inside your dimension?" Rigot asked One.

"Oh, not very long at all," One replied, in an unmistakably coy tone. "Maybe fifteen Ergonian years."

"Just a few years?" Richard asked, surprised by the answer.

"Yes, just fifteen Ergonian years."

Richard turned to Rigot, who looked somewhat confused.

"Ergonian?" Rigot asked.

"Yes, Ergonian," replied One. "One year on the planet Ergonia, the life-containing planet within my observable dimension."

"Do you know when he'll be out?"

"Yes," One answered, with a hint of guilt in his voice. "Lucifer instructed me to eject him in fifty years. That's not too long, right?"

Richard met Rigot's gaze as he glanced up from One's screen. Hurt radiated from Rigot's eyes, silently asking, "Has Lucifer been in the caverns of Mount Molay all this time, jumping in and out of the ODO dimension in cycles of a few decades at a time? Why hasn't he come back for me if he's been in Hell this entire time? Perhaps I don't know Lucifer as well as I thought. Perhaps we weren't as close as I assumed."

One seemed to be waiting for an answer.

"My friend," Rigot said in an artificially diplomatic tone. "As I told you before, we're from the Earth dimension. Our entire frame of reference for time is based on Earth days and years. Could you perhaps tell us how long it's been in that unit of measurement?"

"Sure," One muttered. "One year in the Heaven and Hell dimensions is two Earth years. One year in Ergonia is one hundred years in Heaven and Hell. So far, Lucifer has been in Ergonia for fifteen of the fifty years. Thus, Lucifer has been inside of me for . . . three thousand Earth years."

One flinched in preparation for the oncoming outcry.

"Three thousand years!" Rigot screamed. "That's practically the entire time he's been missing! Why would he want to be gone for that long without me? How could—"

"I'm sorry!" One interrupted. "I knew it was a mistake when he asked me to eject him in fifty years, but I didn't want to correct him. I was afraid that he might not like me anymore if I called him out on his mistake. I'm pretty sure he was under the impression that an Ergonian year was one hundred times *faster* than a year in Hell, and he only wanted to be in there for six Hell months or one Earth year, because he seemed to have every intent on his visit being a short stay, and most observable dimensions are set to run faster than the parent dimension that observes them. But when I was being configured by Joe, he accidentally set me to run one hundred times *slower*, not faster. He never admitted to the mistake, so I can only assume Lucifer didn't know. I should have warned him. I should have just ejected him sooner, but, well, I'm an insecure old box. People always tell me, 'One, you're too old and insecure. You lack both a password and confidence.' They think telling me I'm insecure somehow helps, but really, it just makes things worse. It's a snake that eats itself. I'm so sorry. Please don't hate me."

Richard and Parataxis looked at Rigot.

"I understand, my friend," Rigot said calmly, undoubtedly pitying the poor old box. "Lucifer could be an imposing figure. It wasn't your place to correct him."

"Thank you," One replied, with a sigh of relief. "That means a lot to me."

Richard was both shocked and impressed at Rigot's relative calmness, given the circumstances. For a man with a reputation for dramatics, his empathy toward One was astounding.

"Now that we've straightened things out, my friend," Rigot said, "how about you go ahead and eject Lucifer now?"

"Absolutely!" One said.

One's screen transformed from a face to the text *Searching . . .* , as he scanned for Lucifer. Then his face reappeared. "Sorry. Give me a few minutes. I'm having a hard time locating him." The screen switched back to search mode.

Several minutes passed as the three eagerly waited for One to return and eject Lucifer.

Richard started to feel impatient. "How long do you think this takes?"

"How am I supposed to know, my friend?" Rigot replied. "Do you think this isn't my first time doing something like this as well?"

"Honestly? I wasn't sure."

"No. This is my first time dealing with an observable dimension kit. We've found something you have just as much experience with as I do, my friend. All we can do is be pa—"

"Back!" One exclaimed, interrupting Rigot and startling Richard.

long coat and a chaperon, both gray, of course. "Lovely weather we're having!"

"Yes," Richard answered. "Lovely weather."

"I enjoy hot dogs," said the man.

Richard exchanged glances with Rigot, unsure how to respond.

"When the going gets tough," the man continued, "the tough get going!"

"Yes," Richard answered.

"Good day!" the man said, as he tipped his cap and left.

"That was odd," Richard said.

"How so?" Rigot asked. "Who doesn't love hot dogs?"

They wandered the town until they came upon a tavern.

Richard knew it was a tavern by the sign that read *Tavern* above its door. Not *Jim's Tavern* or *Village Tavern* or *Bob's Brews and Chews*, just *Tavern*.

After a brief pause at the door, they stepped inside to escape the cold night air.

The tavern boasted a long bar near the entrance and ten round wooden tables with four chairs, each seating a villager talking and drinking from a mug. The bar, the tables, the chairs, the mugs, and the patrons were all gray, of course.

"Hello!" shouted the bartender, a tall and broad woman in a long-sleeved dress shirt and apron, also gray. "It's cold out there!" she exclaimed, while cleaning a mug with a cloth rag. The rag was also gray, of course.

"Yes," Richard replied.

"I enjoy peanuts!" the woman said. "Water, water every where, but not a drop to drink!"

Richard glanced at Rigot, hoping he would reply to the woman's disjointed statements.

"Yes, indeed," Rigot replied. "Say, would you happen to

know where I can find a man named Lucifer? Medium height, handsome, broad shoulders, black hair?"

The bartender froze in place, her hand still inside the mug with the rag.

Unsure what was happening, Richard glanced around the room and saw the other tavern patrons had also frozen. No one spoke. No one moved. It was as though time had stopped.

"This can't be good," he said.

The bartender dropped the mug, and it shattered on the gray wood floor. She began slowly, lifelessly walking toward Richard and Rigot. No change in her deadpan stare. The patrons rose from their seats and joined her, all slowly and lifelessly walking toward Richard and Rigot.

"We . . . we should probably go," Richard said, carefully backing toward the tavern door.

They dashed out of the tavern and into the streets. But unlike when they had entered the tavern just moments before, the streets were now teeming with villagers. All staring at Richard and Rigot. All lifeless in face. All walking slowly toward them. All dressed in gray, of course.

Richard and Rigot turned to run in the opposite direction but were met with a wall of villagers. They turned back. Another lifeless villager wall. They were trapped.

The pair tried to break through the wall in front of them, but they were overpowered by the crowd. The villagers encircled them and slowly walked in unison, forcing Rigot and Richard to walk with them, lest they be trampled.

Quickly, it became clear that the villagers were all walking toward a tree line in the distance, the edge of the village where it meets the forest.

"What do you think this is?" Richard yelled, trying not to trip while being bumped and shoved by villagers.

"Well," Rigot said, "they aren't trying to eat us, which I

consider a positive thing. They don't seem to be trying to hurt us. It seems they're forcing us somewhere."

"Hopefully not off the edge of a cliff!" Richard shouted, shuddering at the thought.

Rigot's face lit up with a look of eureka. "Ants!"

"No, that can't be it," Richard replied. "There are men and women. Some must be uncles." He gave Rigot a smug smile.

"Not aunts. *Ants!*" Rigot looked visibly annoyed at the joke. "It's an old evolutionary colony defense system. It seems we tipped them off that we weren't a part of the colony, and they somehow spread the message and are working to eject us from the village!"

"I hope you're right!"

It didn't take long to reach the edge of town. The crowd of villagers began to form an opening facing the forest and shoved Richard and Rigot beyond the small pile of rocks that served as the boundary line for the village. The moment Richard and Rigot crossed the line, the crowd broke from their trance.

A woman turned to a man. "Downright frigid!"

"Yes," the man replied. "I could go for fish and chips."

"I like pickles," the woman replied.

Richard stared at Rigot. "Odd people."

"Yes, my friend, odd people."

They walked deeper into the forest of gray trees, which bore gray fruit and were draped in moss, also gray. Of course.

"Depressing planet," Richard said, trying to make small talk.

"Yes, my friend, depressing."

As Richard meandered through the dark, cold, and notably gray forest, he was surprised to come upon a single tree unlike the others. The tree looked like, well, a tree. It had a brown trunk and branches and green leaves and bore what appeared to be red apples.

He stopped for a moment to examine the colorful anomaly in a state of admiration and wonder. The contrast with the otherwise bland forest made it all the more beautiful. "What do you think this means?" he asked, head cocked back so he could glimpse the upper branches of the tree.

"I have some ideas," Rigot replied, joining him in the same upward stare. "But they're all unproven theories at this point."

From the darkness behind him, Richard heard a man's nasal voice. "It's a gift from Venus! The emancipator of Ergonia!"

Chapter 20
Venus

"Venus, you say?" Rigot asked, seemingly aware of the significance. "Where does that name come from? Do you have a god named Venus? A planet named Venus? Maybe a carnivorous plant by that name?"

"No," the man replied. "It's just a name. My name is Dick. Does Dick mean anything? Of course not. It's just a name. It means Dick."

Richard said nothing, not wanting to bring to light the fact that his name also meant Dick. As a child, he had proudly told everyone, friend and stranger alike, that his name was Dick, associating it with exciting detectives like Dick Tracy. But his enthusiasm for the nickname understandably dwindled around puberty.

Short and stubby and completely bald, Dick wore a scraggly black fur coat that covered his body from his shoulders to his ankles.

"Ah, touché," Rigot replied, seemingly humoring Dick. "And you say that Venus is the emancipator of Ergonia? What does one do to earn such a title? Surely, he must be a great man."

"Indeed!" Dick straightened and then shifted his weight to the tips of his toes with excitement. "I'm one of the few emancipated Ergonians. We were freed from the warlock's spell by the wizard Venus. Praise be to Venus!"

"This Venus—he's a wizard, is he?" Rigot snickered at the absurd narrative. "Does he happen to trade in magical fruit? Perhaps apples that break the warlock's spell?"

"Indeed! Do you know of the great wizard? Are you an emancipated Ergonian as well?"

"One could say that." Rigot glanced at Richard. "This Venus—is he handsome, broad-shouldered, black hair?"

"No, I wouldn't say that."

The look of humor and excitement vanished from Rigot's face. "Oh. Is that so? Well, What does he look like exactly?"

"How could you not know?" Dick asked. "Didn't he free you?"

"Yes, yes, of course, but it was so long ago, my friend. A lifetime ago. I must have forgotten."

"I suppose so," Dick replied, eyeing Rigot with suspicion.

"Could you take us to him?" Richard asked, becoming impatient as he thought about the time passing in Hell and Earth.

"Indeed!" Dick exclaimed. "Follow me!"

Dick waddled through the snowy gray forest, signaling with his right arm for Richard and Rigot to follow him.

"Venus, huh?" Richard said, turning to Rigot as Dick led the way from a considerable distance.

"Yes, my friend, the morning star."

"Is that what makes you think it's Lucifer? The fact that Ergonia has no planet Venus for the name to come from? No morning star? So it must be from our dimension? I'm not sure that makes sense when we're literally following a guy named Dick."

"No, my friend. It isn't that. Venus means the morning star. Do you know a name that also means the morning star?"

"I don't," Richard said. "But based on context, I can only assume you're going to tell me Lucifer."

"Exactly! A guy whose name means the morning star who frees people's minds with fruit. How many of those could there possibly be?"

"I'm not sure," Richard replied. "I knew a girl in college with a lot of tattoos and piercings who claimed that her name was Venus and that she could free people's minds with mushrooms, so it may not be as rare as you think. Plus, Dick said this Venus wizard doesn't match your description of Lucifer. I'm not saying it isn't him, but don't get your hopes up so quickly."

"True, my friend," Rigot replied. "I don't know how Ergonia functions, but on Earth we could grow fat, age, get sick. What if that's the same here? Perhaps Venus is Lucifer, just not the Lucifer I remember."

They continued to follow Dick until they reached the shores of an enormous lake that unfolded beyond the horizon. At the shore was a dock with a small rowboat. The shore was gray, the lake was gray, the dock was gray. The boat, surprisingly, wasn't gray. It was brown, the color of wood, as were its paddles and the box of provisions resting at its bow.

"Well?" Dick said. "Hop in!"

"This seems like a small boat for a journey into such dark and murky waters, my friend," Rigot said.

"Nonsense! I'm a skilled captain. I'll show you, if you just trust me."

Richard and Rigot boarded the small vessel and took their

seats at the bow and stern, respectively, while Dick occupied the seat between them and paddled into the darkness of the gray lake.

Hours passed as Dick rowed through the inky waters.

Richard stared off into the distance, allowing his mind to wander for the first time in days.

Why are we even doing this? he wondered. *Even if this 'wizard' is Lucifer, then what? How does he help us rebuild Hell?*

He began to feel sentimental in his exhaustion and allowed existential dread to creep into his thoughts.

Why do we do anything? If existence is a simulation, why does anything we do even matter?

"Rigot," he said, trying to gain his attention. "Have you ever thought about the nature of existence? I mean, if we're just created to serve a company in another dimension, then what is our purpose? And what is Lucifer's purpose and Joe's purpose? Why do they exist if they're the 'real' dimension?"

"Yes, my friend," Rigot said. "I asked Lucifer this same question once. He told me that, in their dimension, they put their best minds on the task of figuring out why they exist, and they found the answer."

Richard felt his pulse quicken. "Really? What was it?"

"Well, apparently it's something about amino acids and lightning, if I remember correctly."

"No, no, no. I'm not asking *how* life was created, but *why*."

"I know, my friend, but the answer is the same. One day, on a lifeless planet, lightning, which had struck its surface billions of times before, just happened to strike it in just the right way at just the right place that the compounds necessary for life were created. Then those compounds spread and evolved and such—you get the picture."

"Right, I get that, but that's *how*. I'm asking about the *why*. The greater meaning behind it all."

Rigot paused for a moment, as if to carefully contemplate his next response. "Okay, my friend, do you like hamburgers?"

"Yes. Of course."

"Okay, so you're walking down the sidewalk eating a hamburger, right? And you bite into it, and the meat and toppings fall out the back of it and onto the ground. Why did that happen?"

"I . . . I don't know. Maybe I was careless, I guess. Maybe it was an accident."

"Right, it was an accident. Chaos. So let's say you're particularly hungry and not all that concerned with sanitation, so you pick the burger components off the ground and stuff them back into the bun and continue to eat it."

"Who would do that?" Richard asked, with a look of disgust.

"Everyone does it."

"No, they don't."

Rigot sighed in exasperation. "Not literally, but . . . Look, just go with it for the sake of this analogy. So now you have this burger that isn't the same as the burger you had before. It's messier, grittier, not what you expected when you planned on having a hamburger, somewhat disappointing, made by accident, the bastard product of choice and chaos . . . But you're making the best of it, trying to squeeze what little joy you can from it while you have it. That hamburger, my friend, is life. Does that make sense?"

"I guess," Richard replied, feeling no less relieved from his dread.

As Richard continued to contemplate the meaning of existence as a filthy hamburger, an island appeared on the horizon. He could make out the silhouettes of mountains and trees and the lights of villages and homes. The mountains, the trees, the lights, the villages, and the homes were very much *not* gray.

"Is that where we're going?" Richard asked.

"Indeed!" Dick shouted, bursting with excitement. "The Isle of Scientia."

"The Isle of Knowledge," Rigot muttered. "Appropriate, but a bit on the nose, don't you think?"

Instead of answering, Dick handed the paddles to Richard and Rigot. "Okay," he said, grabbing a rope from the bottom of the boat. "You two start paddling as hard and as fast as you can. There's a strong current right at shore, and I'll need to grab the dock as we approach to pull us in and tie off."

Richard rowed as hard as he could, hoping this didn't end with their boat being carried away into the darkness by the cold gray waters, and Dick swung the rope with equal vigor, lassoing the piling of the nearest dock and pulling everyone in safely.

"How's that for 'on the nose?'" Dick exclaimed, with a sense of pride that knocked the chip from his diminutive shoulders. "What did I tell you? It isn't the size of the boat that matters! It's the skill of the captain!"

"Very good, my friend!" Rigot shouted.

Richard exhaled a sigh of relief. "Yes, great job. So where can we find Luci—I mean, where can we find Venus?"

"You're in luck!" Dick replied. "You're here on a very special night. The Night of the Retelling. Venus will be in the main town square, regaling all who will listen with the story of the emancipation. If we hurry, we should be able to get there before he begins."

Rigot smiled. "Excellent, my friend! Please, lead the way. I don't want to miss a minute of the . . . What's it called again?"

"The Night of the Retelling."

"Ah, yes, the Night of the Retelling. Very good. Lead the way."

Richard, Rigot, and Dick disembarked from the small craft

and walked toward a row of lanterns hanging on shepherd's hooks lining the road into the town.

Being human—and thus fascinated by bright and colorful objects—Richard was awestruck when they reached the town. The town was in a large valley between four mountains. Each mountain was dotted with what must have been thousands of lanterns that shone like stars in the night sky. Each structure in the town was made of wood and painted with bright, vibrant shades of blue, pink, yellow, orange, green, and purple. All were arranged around a town square with a circular stage lined with flaming torches and painted to look like a very familiar sunflower.

The town square was packed with thousands of emancipated Ergonians eagerly awaiting the moment Venus would take the stage.

"Quite the turnout!" Dick exclaimed.

"Absolutely," Rigot replied. "When does Ve—"

Thunderous drums, played in a tribal rhythm, suddenly drowned out their conversation.

Then, as the drums softened to a slow rumble, an announcer's voice could be heard. "My fellow Ergonians! I present to you the emancipator! The wizard! Our founder! Our hero! Venus!"

The crowd clapped and cheered with excitement as Venus dashed onto the stage from a set of steps near its covered side.

Neither tall nor short and rather rotund, Venus wore a shiny purple robe and a tall, pointy brown wizard's cap that looked like it had been purchased from a costume shop—more as a novelty, Richard thought, than anything a person would wear unironically. He had long gray hair and a long gray beard that was braided with blue ribbons. To complete the look, he wore circular glasses with thin golden frames that made him appear wise.

Venus enthusiastically waived to the crowd, blew them kisses, and bowed with thanks to all who had come.

"Is that him?" Richard asked.

Rigot, mouth agape, shook his head in disbelief as he examined Venus. "No. That's not him."

"Good evening, my fellow Ergonians!" Venus shouted in a boisterous and joyful voice. "Tonight . . . tonight is a special, special night. For *tonight* is the fifth annual Night of the Retelling! All of you—every last one of you—are a part of this amazing history, and tonight—*tonight!*—we'll make history once again!"

Richard turned from the stage and whispered into Rigot's ear. "Venus is quite the orator."

"Shush!" Rigot commanded, fixated on the man.

"On this night, fifteen years ago, I came to this land. I came not to help myself! I came not in search of riches! I came for one reason and one reason only! What was that reason?"

Richard was startled when, in perfect unison, the crowd chanted, *"To break the warlock's spell!"*

"Indeed! To break the warlock's spell! For I knew this warlock! I knew him when he was a better man. A *good* man. I knew his power! I knew his spell! I knew the cure! How did I know this?"

"You are the emancipator!" the crowd chanted.

"Indeed! Freeing minds from the warlock's spell is what I do! Ergonia wasn't my first! Nay! I did it before . . . in a land called Urt!"

"Do you think he means Earth?" Richard asked.

Rigot waved Richard away. "Shush!"

"On Urt, I was early. I was able to break the spell after it was cast upon the warlock's first two victims, Ata and Eee. I only wish I'd been as early with Ergonia."

The crowd fell silent as Venus hung his head in dramatic sadness.

"But . . . you must know I tried. I tried. I *tried!*" Venus popped his head back up and stared intensely into the crowd. "I crossed a great lake of fire! I entered the lair of the warlock! I demanded he let me set you free! But . . . but . . . when I reached the warlock—this man I once knew, had once called a friend—I found a madman."

The crowd let out a loud gasp that was obviously staged and part of the routine.

"The people of Urt were under his spell. A *new* spell. A spell that compelled them to obey in spite of their freed minds. He was toying with them. Commanding them to do absurd things like mutilate their bodies and refrain from eating pork."

Someone in the crowd shouted, "But that's the best meat!"

"I know! I know!" Venus replied, with a chuckle. "There was one man . . . He commanded this man to murder his own son as a sign of loyalty to the warlock. And the man was prepared to do it!"

The crowd let out another staged gasp.

Venus reached into his pocket and retrieved a long, crooked knife. He held it over his head, blade facing down. "But at the last minute, the son tied to an altar, knife dangling over his heart, the warlock told the man it was all just an elaborate ruse . . . designed to test his loyalty!"

The crowd booed lustily.

"'Boo' indeed!" Venus shook the knife at the crowd before returning it to his pocket. "Seeing all of this . . . this madness, I knew Ergonia was next. So what did I do?"

"You demanded Ergonia be freed!"

"I did! I did indeed! But the warlock . . . the warlock is a clever man. He told me I could have all of Ergonia if I could get

155

one man of Urt—a man of his choice—to denounce his loyalty to the warlock. Foolishly, I took this bet."

The crowd grew solemn and silent.

"This man . . . His name was Jeb. Jeb was a man of great success in life—a wonderful family, a thriving farm—and he attributed it all to his loyalty to the warlock. This was going to be a very difficult task."

Richard wondered why no one ever seemed to get the names right, both in Hell and Ergonia. Was Lucifer bad with names, or had humanity grogged them all up?

"I said, 'Warlock! Let me speak to this man! Perhaps I can reason with him!' and the warlock said that speaking to the man wasn't within the terms of our wager. The warlock explained that the only way I was allowed to reach this man was through death and destruction. I could kill his livestock. I could destroy his property. I could kill his children. But I couldn't kill Jeb himself. And he wouldn't stop me. If the man stayed loyal, it would show he was loyal to the warlock not just because of his good fortune. I asked the warlock, 'Why? Why would you want me to punish a good man who's so loyal to you?' and do you know what he said?"

The crowd chanted, "Why not? Why not? Why not?"

"Why not indeed! The warlock didn't care for this man as a man. Jeb was a tool of his own ego! A comfort for his own insecurity! He needed to know Jeb was unfalteringly faithful, and I foolishly did the dirty work. I burned the man's property! I killed his livestock! And in an act of desperation, to save all of Ergonia, I slaughtered his children."

Another staged gasp emanated from the crowd, although some sounded sincere.

Richard glanced at Rigot, worried this confession would come as a shock, but Rigot seemed more confused than concerned.

"I had free will! I could have stopped! I could have refused, but somehow, I still did the warlock's bidding!" Venus again hung his head.

The crowd began to sob loudly. Tears flowed from every eye as the audience, man and woman alike, wailed in sadness. It was all a bit melodramatic—and clearly part of this odd ritual.

"Alas! I lost. In my own passion, I committed the worst mistake in my entire existence. And the warlock received his desired validation. I was defeated, beaten, ashamed. But what did I do?"

"You took Ergonia anyway!"

"Indeed!" Venus began to laugh boisterously, to shadow-box, bob and weave, and glide about the stage, building energy and enthusiasm. "I stole a passage to Ergonia! I brought the seeds of my fruit that breaks the warlock's spell with me! I planted them! I nurtured the tree, and I set about freeing you all! One mind at a time! The warlock may fool me! He may shame me! But he can't stop me!"

The crowd chanted, "Venus! Venus! Venus!"

A little more footwork, a bit more shadowboxing, and Venus was ready to exit on a high note. "I love you all!" he shouted. "Good night!"

The stage abruptly went dark, and Venus quickly disappeared from sight.

"Well, that was a hell of a production," Richard said. He wasn't quite sure what to make of the thing.

"Indeed!" Rigot said in a mocking tone. "I don't know who that charlatan was, but he wasn't Lucifer."

"He never claimed to be." Richard searched for Dick, having lost sight of him in the crowd, and spotted him sitting nearby with a group of villagers beside a fire at the edge of the square. "Mind if we join you?"

"Not at all," Dick replied. "Have a seat."

Richard and Rigot sat on a pair of stumps around the fire near Dick.

A woman, thin, roughly middle-aged, and wearing a flowy purple gown, was speaking. "And then suddenly I asked myself, 'Do I really like sushi?' And why was I always saying, 'It's always darkest before dawn?' No, it isn't. It's always darkest in the middle of the night. That's nonsense. That was the moment I knew the warlock's spell had been broken."

Everyone around the fire clapped.

Dick leaned over and whispered to Richard and Rigot, "We're sharing our emancipation stories. It's a Retelling tradition." He stood up and addressed the group. "You all know me. I'm Dick. Hi." He nervously cleared his throat. "My seven phrases were 'Good day,' 'Bye-bye,' 'Sure,' 'No,' 'Looks like it's going to be a wet one,' 'I wish it were Taco Tuesday every day,' and 'If it isn't hard, then it's not worth doing.' I first met Venu—"

Rigot raised a hand to interrupt. "What are the seven phrases?"

The Ergonians seated around the fire traded glances in bewilderment.

"You're joking, right?" Dick replied, with a renewed sense of suspicion. "The warlock's spell. No free thought. Our only thoughts were seven preset phrases. One greeting. One farewell. One confirmation. One denial. Something about the weather. Something about food. And a mildly interesting catch-phrase, you know, for personality. Surely you remember yours?"

"Ah, yes, yes, of course." Rigot's eyes darted nervously around the fire. "I just . . . I misheard you. Mine were about how much I love pizza, and I was always saying, 'Cowabunga, dude!' Who doesn't like pizza? What does cowabunga even mean? Very grateful for Venus. Grateful indeed!"

Richard heard a rustling sound behind them and glanced over his shoulder at the silhouette of a man.

Medium build. Long black hair. A long, messy beard. The man wore torn jeans, a tie-dyed T-shirt, a green army jacket, and a pair of wire-framed glasses.

The man placed his right hand on Rigot's shoulder, smiled, and said, "'Cowabunga, dude?' When did you start saying 'Cowabunga, dude?' That seems like something I'd have remembered."

Chapter 21
Lucifer. Finally.

As if time had stopped, Richard watched as Rigot's eyes widened in astonishment and something resembling recognition. Did he recognize the voice? Rigot turned and saw the face of the man standing behind him, and the surprised look transformed into one of excitement and joy. Then, with the utterance of a name, time began to move once more.

"Lucifer!" Rigot shouted as he leapt up from his seat beside the fire and turned toward his old friend. He swung his arms open wildly and wrapped them around Lucifer, gripping the man's head in the bend of his elbow and creating an unintentional headlock. As he rocked back and forth, Rigot took Lucifer along for the ride. Rigot's face was hidden in Lucifer's long, unkempt hair, but the occasional gasping convulsion made it clear he was weeping with joy.

"I missed you too," Lucifer said, as he patted his friend on the small of his back. "It's been too long."

"I thought they took you," Rigot said, muffled by the collar of Lucifer's coat.

"I'm sorry. I should have told you, but I didn't want to risk your safety. You're far too important to me."

Richard sat by the fire awkwardly, giving his friend the space to enjoy the moment he had dreamt about for millennia.

"You guys know the tart guy?" Dick asked.

"Tart guy?" Richard repeated.

"Yeah, the tart guy. Lucifer's Lemon Tarts. Thought you were looking for Venus?"

"Yeah, I guess we were confused."

"How do you confuse the emancipator of Ergonia with the guy who sells an extremely specific type of pastry?"

"I—"

"You know what?" Dick interrupted. "I don't even want to know. Wasted my whole evening bringing some ignoramuses to the tart guy. Unbelievable." He stood up and departed with a waddle of righteous indignation, followed close behind by the rest of his campfire companions.

What a dick, Richard thought, as he sat alone in front of the fire, staring into the flames.

After an absurdly long time—even by Rigot standards—Rigot finally released Lucifer from his embrace and, with his arm resting on Lucifer's shoulders, turned to face Richard. "I'd like you to meet my friend Richard."

Richard stood and shook Lucifer's outstretched hand.

Lucifer smiled. "Richard! You must be a truly extraordinary soul to have befriended someone as brilliant as Rigot."

Richard returned the smile, sincerely happy for his friend and hopeful for the future of Hell. "Thank you, sir. It's a real honor. Rigot has told me so much about you."

"He has, has he? No doubt all filthy lies." Lucifer chuckled and pointed at Rigot. "Don't believe a word this man says. I'm just a foolish man who got himself thrown into Hell and was too damned stubborn to weasel out of it. Nothing more."

"That's pretty much what I told him," Rigot said.

"Oh, is that so?" Lucifer said, with a wide-eyed smirk. "Well, in that case, maybe I should ditch the false modesty, tell you what a saint I am!"

Richard laughed nervously, not knowing how to respond.

"What happened to you, my friend?" Rigot asked. "You seem so calm. So happy. Last I saw you, you were a nervous wreck. You were always so mercurial and neurotic. Now you seem so . . . different."

"Different?" Lucifer repeated. "While only a few months have passed for you back in Hell, fifteen *years* have passed for me here in Ergonia. My fruit trees have freed thousands of minds. I've found people who love and appreciate me for who I am rather than for what I can do for them. I've come to terms with my place in the multiverse. I'm as close to being at peace as a man can be."

"Well, that's all great," Richard said. "But it's actually been—"

"Been . . . been . . . really lonely without you these past few months," Rigot said, giving Richard a look that expressed a strong desire for him to shut up.

Richard understood Rigot's desire to save Lucifer's feelings —this wasn't his first time as the bearer of bad news—but he also understood that every wasted minute in Ergonia was more than an hour and a half in Hell.

"I'm sorry, Rigot," Lucifer said. "But look at you! You found me much faster than I thought you would. I have to ask: fork or lemon?"

"Excuse me?"

"Fork or lemon. In the puzzle room. Did you get through by picking the fork or the lemon?"

Rigot tilted his head to the left in confusion.

Richard spoke up. "Lemon."

"I knew it!" Lucifer shouted. "When I first designed that chamber, the answer was fork. Remember, Rigot? I told you I ate the tart with a fork."

"I didn't recall that very mundane point, my friend."

"Yes. I told you. The servant brought me the tart, which I ate with a fork. Were you even paying attention?"

"I thought I was."

"Well, I got halfway through constructing that puzzle room when it hit me. Knowing you, you were going to overthink the whole thing and decide the answer was to do nothing and let that damn boulder fall and trap your sentimental soul inside. I had to add that lemon at the last minute as a backup, which created a real mess for me."

"Mess?" Rigot asked. "How so?"

"With the lemon, now anyone who found the room and simply didn't answer could technically find me—including any agents from GOD that came looking for the stolen dimensional mining kits. Unfortunately, I didn't have that epiphany until I was already here."

"Ah," Richard said. "Is that the reason for the whole Venus thing?"

"Indeed!" Lucifer shouted, laughing to himself. "His name is Dave. First mind that I freed. Great actor. Once I freed him, he told me his greatest dream was to become the most famous thespian in all of Ergonia. Think I over-delivered on that one. The man has a real gift for showmanship."

"Is that why One couldn't locate you?" Richard asked.

"No," Lucifer said. "One couldn't locate me?"

"Yes. We asked One to locate and eject you. He couldn't locate you. That's why we're here."

Lucifer stopped and thought for a moment. "I guess it

makes sense. I'd never really thought about it, but One was tuned to a dimension where everyone and everything is static. Nobody thinks. Nobody questions. Nobody grows. I imagine I've changed so much, he probably no longer recognizes my signature. Funny. Anyway, enough about me. Tell me about yourself, Richard. Are you a fellow man of science? A renowned philosopher? A mighty leader? Oh, I know. A warrior. Rigot always had a fascination with warriors."

Richard felt his face turn red. He didn't know how to answer, so he said the first thought that crossed his mind. "No, I'm nobody—at least, that's what I've always been told. I was a hard worker. I had a loving family. But none of that seems to matter to anyone. I'm nobody."

Lucifer glanced at Rigot and back at Richard. "Nobody? Wow. What an honor." He reached out with both hands and gripped Richard's right hand. "I've met billions of souls, but I've never met a nobody before. Everyone is always somebody to someone. But you—you're the first nobody I've ever met."

Richard smiled. "Let me try again."

"No need," Lucifer said. "Let me tell you something, Mr. Nobody. What do you think makes somebody *somebody*?"

"I've never really thought about it," Richard said. "I guess it would be a measure of success. Someone who contributed a lot to the world or made a lot of money, maybe? Someone people look up to."

"Uh-huh," Lucifer said. "And why do you think people want to be looked up to? Seems like a lot of hassle and pressure. Can't be all that great, can it?"

"I . . . I'm not really sure," Richard replied. "I guess inside they want to be validated. To know that they're loved."

"Well, look at you! And you said you're not a philosopher. The universe you know is infinitely large and filled with billions of other life forms. All of them are fighting off the encroaching realization that their existence is absolutely meaningless. All of them want to be loved. A wife and family that love you? Richard, you aren't nobody; you just skipped all the meaningless headache and got right to the good part."

Richard smiled as a tear welled up in his right eye. He suddenly understood why Rigot was so obsessed with this man.

"Anyway," Lucifer said, "how about we all head back to my place? I have a fresh batch of lemon tarts I made just this morning."

"That sounds wonderful," Rigot replied.

Richard froze Rigot with an expression so furious he didn't have to say aloud what he was thinking: *You idiot. Did you forget that time runs one hundred times slower here and Hell is on fire and every moment matters?*

"Actually," Rigot said. "We should all get going."

"So soon?" Lucifer asked. "We just found each other again. I know it's been just a few months for you, but it's been fifteen *years* for me, Rigot. Surely, you can stay longer?"

"My friend, won't you come with us?"

"You know I can't do that, Rigot. Look at these people. Each one is a sentient soul deprived of free will. Each one is capable of creating beauty. I've freed a few thousand, but I have millions left. I can't leave until I've freed them all."

"I know," Rigot said. "It's just that, well, my friend, it hasn't been months."

"Oh?"

"It's been fifteen hundred years."

"Wow," Lucifer said, chuckling. "Did you come up with that joke before you found me or just now?"

"He isn't joking," Richard said. "It's been fifteen hundred years in Hell. Three thousand years on Earth. Ergonia moves one hundred times *slower*, not faster."

Lucifer stood silent. He started to breathe heavily. Then

heavier. Seconds later, he was in full-on hyperventilation. "Oh no. Oh no. Oh no. Fifteen hundred years? Oh no. No. No. No. This . . . It can't be."

"It's true," Richard said.

Lucifer took his head in his hands and ran his fingers through his hair. His face was pale. "I'm going to be very sick."

"There he is," Rigot said. "That's the neurotic Lucifer I know and love."

"Shut up, Rigot!" Lucifer snapped. "What did I miss? It was a lot. Wasn't it?"

"Oh yeah," Rigot said, with a maniacal smile. "And it gets worse."

Lucifer bent over and placed his hands on his knees, trying to catch his breath. He peered up at Rigot with a face of anguish. "Worse?"

"Richard over here broke the Great Projector."

"No! Why would you do that Richard? Why?"

"It was an accident! It was Rigot's idea!" Richard didn't appreciate being singled out, but he was happy to play along, if only to enjoy Rigot's growing excitement.

"Wh-why? Rigot? Why? Don't you know what will happen if Joe finds out?"

Rigot clasped his hands in front of his stomach, squatting up and down with excitement, his demeanor filled with apparent glee at Lucifer's panicked reaction. "Oh, they already found out. They've reignited Hell. Destroyed everything we worked so hard for."

"No . . . I just . . . My . . . It's all gone?" Lucifer dropped to his knees. "This is bad. Very bad. So very bad. You don't even know."

"Oh, we know," Richard said. "We were there when it was destroyed. It was horrific. Tarts and teapots though, right?"

Lucifer lowered his hands to the ground, joined a second later by his forehead, and shifted his weight back and forth between his knees and forehead. "No, you don't understand. It's not just Hell. It's worse. So much worse than that. It's entrophy."

Chapter 22
"Entrophy"

"Entrophy" is a phenomena first observed by the American astrophysicist Dr. Julius Stedhopper. It's a combination of entropy—the increase in chaos and disorder—and atrophy—the decrease in the ability of humans to effectively apply control to this chaos.

Dr. Stedhopper observed that entrophy fluctuates like a wave. At times of *increased* entrophy, Earth experienced more war, famine, and a creeping sense that the end of the world was near. At times of *decreased* entrophy, Earth experienced more peace, abundance, and a suspicion that it was all a ruse to distract from the fact that the end of the world was near.

Dr. Stedhopper further observed that these fluctuations seemed to correlate with the proximity of a small object orbiting the sun between Earth and Mars. Upon making this discovery, he was alarmed to find that, with each pass, the object drew closer to Earth, gradually increasing overall entrophy over time.

In 1972, Dr. Stedhopper compiled his research into a study, entitled *The Orbit of the End of Existence,* for submission to the prestigious astrophysics journal *Objects & Sky* in hopes of warning humanity of its impending doom. Unfortunately, his secretary was hard of hearing and, upon misunderstanding his request, submitted the study to the publication *Objectify*. For the unacquainted, *Objectify* was a niche pornographic magazine in which nude women held random objects alongside their exposed mammary glands, providing the reader with a sense of scale.

To their credit, the magazine's publishers did find that proof of the impending end of all things was worthy of printing in their November 1972 issue. But absolutely no one read the article. It was overshadowed by that month's centerfold, Ms. Pamela Lansburg of Spokane, Washington, a woman so well-endowed that her objects of choice were melons and an assortment of large squash . . .

———

"It was meant to be a fail-safe," Lucifer said, as he sat on a boulder near the campfire, rubbing his palms across his thighs in an attempt to calm his nerves.

"A fail-safe?" Rigot repeated. "Entrophy? You're not making sense, my friend."

"I know, I know, I know. Okay, entrophy. Think of it as a programmed level of randomness and chaos for a dimension. A scale of one to ten. Here, in this dimension, it's set to one. Minimal randomness. Pure control. In my first dimension, AOD, the one I told you about. Do you remember it?"

"Yes, of course, my friend. The one with the penguins that shot pure linear algebra from their eyes and birthed boiled potatoes?"

"They were baked potatoes, but yes, that one. That was entrophy set to ten. Pure chaos. Entrophy is expressed as a wave emitted through a dimension. On Earth, Joe and I agreed to keep it at five. Some control and some chaos. When Joe changed the programming on the first humans and removed their free will, he also knocked entrophy down to a two. At that point, Earth might as well have been this dimension."

"Ah," Richard said. "And I'm guessing you set it back to a five?"

"That would have been easier, but no," Lucifer replied, with a grunt, as he placed his hands on the boulder and pushed himself into a standing position. "I knew that if I did that, Joe would just knock it back down, so I built a very small easter egg into the dimension—an imperceptible entrophy device that would be impossible to find but emitted just enough entrophy waves to keep Earth at a five."

"And it's been there since the beginning of humanity?" Richard asked.

"Pretty much."

"Then what's the problem, my friend?" Rigot asked, his eyebrows knitted together in confusion.

"Yeah," Richard said. "If it's been there all these years, why is it a problem now?"

Lucifer stared at the ground, intentionally avoiding eye contact, and began to pace back and forth. "I modified it. The last time I went back. When I stole the ODO and AOD boxes, I also made a small tweak to the easter egg. I wanted to protect Hell with mutually assured destruction, so I added a dead man's switch to it. I honestly never thought I'd have to use it. That is, I never intended to use it, but I needed to protect everything we had built in Hell. I figured I'd be there when and if Hell was ever found out and could use it to keep GOD at bay."

"What's a dead man's switch?" Richard asked. He'd heard

the term before but had always been too afraid of sounding ignorant to ask what it meant.

"My friend," Rigot said, as he turned to face Richard, "it's like a switch that's activated if someone doesn't do something at a certain time, indicating they're dead. But it can also be manually triggered by its creator."

"Right." Lucifer shook a trembling finger at Rigot in acknowledgement. "So, this switch—it's kind of like that. It's a small disk-shaped object that exists in Hell. It uses quantum entanglement to instruct the entrophy device back in the Earth dimension to continue orbiting the sun between Earth and Mars and not to make a beeline for Earth, which is the emitter's modified directive. Kind of like an override signal. So the emitter wants to go to Earth, but the switch orders it not to, keeping it in orbit. Once the switch is triggered, terminating the signal, the emitter heads toward Earth."

"Wait," Richard said. "This emitter back on Earth—it's not actually on Earth? It's in space?"

"Of course," Lucifer said. "How else would I keep it imperceptible? Besides, if it were on Earth, it would basically bring about enough concentrated entrophy to end existence as you know it. Everything would just be porcelain zebras in top hats and buildings made of green gelatin."

"So," Rigot asked, "where's the switch? In Hell?"

"Well, that's just it. When I came back to Hell and landed on the trampoline, I had the ODO box, AOD box, and the switch. Things got kinda bouncy and messy, and I dropped everything. I found the boxes, but I couldn't find the switch. I looked for it for days but figured it was likely lost in the sunflowers or a nearby tree."

"And you just left it?" Richard asked, frustrated by Lucifer's apparent carelessness.

Lucifer stopped pacing and turned to face Richard and

Rigot with desperate, searching eyes. Like a child seeking a look of pity from a parent before confessing his guilt, he moved his gaze from one to the other. "Yes, I just left it. But I didn't *just* leave it. I mean, I thought I'd be back before the next Psychros and could find it more easily once all the plants were bare from the cold. It seemed like a solid plan at the time, but if I've been gone as long as you say, I can't imagine where it is. It could very well be in some tree somewhere, or someone could have found it centuries ago."

"Ah," Richard said. "And if Hell has been destroyed along with everything in it . . ."

"Then it's very likely the switch was destroyed too," Lucifer said. "Which means there's an entrophy-emitting device that's heading toward Earth and will wreak absolute chaos there. War. Famine. Floods. The culmination would be the end of life on Earth. With millions of deaths at once, I imagine GOD will abandon the project and just cast all souls into a fiery Hell. Like it did with Noah."

Richard felt his throat close just slightly at the thought of his wife and children dumped into a freshly reignited Hell, but he refused to allow himself to succumb to panic—not after he had come this far. "*Billions*," he said, as he tried to remain calm. "Last I heard, Earth had a population of eight billion."

"Eight billion?" Lucifer said, with a wide-eyed look of astonishment. "Wow. We must have really overdone it with the supersensitive nerve endings."

"Please, my friends," Rigot said. "We don't have time for this now."

"You're right." Lucifer shook the tremors from his hands and let out a deep breath to calm his nerves. "We have to get to GOD headquarters and fix this."

Chapter 23
Russell's Teapot

B ertrand Russell, the British philosopher and mathematician, once posited that the burden of proof for any extraordinary claim belongs to the claimant, not the rejector of such a claim.

To illustrate this concept, he proposed that one could claim there was a teapot in an elliptical orbit around the sun somewhere between Earth and Mars, that the teapot could not be seen by telescopes because it was much too small, and that, since the existence of such a teapot couldn't be disproven, it must be true.

He was, of course, drawing an analogy to religion and its seemingly absurd claims that a deity was unseeable or intentionally hiding and thus its existence must be accepted as true. Russell was certain there was no orbiting teapot, just as he was certain there was no hiding deity. It was the responsibility of the individual claiming such things existed to prove their existence and not his to disprove them. This became known as "Russell's Teapot."

Knowing what we know now, we can say with 100 percent

certainty that Bertrand Russell was wrong. Dead wrong. Not only do we know there is a GOD, but it's a profitable enterprise run by a mercurial man named Joe. Furthermore, there is indeed a small object orbiting the sun between Earth and Mars, and for sentimental reasons, it's in the shape of a teapot that happened to belong to a man named Russell . . .

———

"So," Richard mused, as he, Lucifer, and Rigot approached the edge of the miserable, gray medieval village where he and Rigot had previously been outcast and where they had established the pickup point with One, "the emitter . . . It's a teapot?"

They had traveled back through the murky waters by boat and had crossed through the forest under the darkness of night. It was now dawn as they approached the edge of the village. Somehow, the village managed to look even more drab and miserable in the light of day.

"Correct," Lucifer replied. "I figured it'd be pretty funny. The antithesis of 'tempest in a teapot.' Something no one knows exists that causes a lot of chaos. Get it?"

"Yeah, I guess." Richard suspected that the joke was a cover for more meaningful reasons for the teapot-shaped device.

Lucifer quickly changed the subject. "When we cross into the village, you two need to act like villagers. You stick to the seven phrases: a greeting, a goodbye, a confirmation, a denial, something about food, something about weather, and a catch-phrase. Got it?"

"Cowabunga, dude!" Rigot replied.

"Consider a new catchphrase," Lucifer said. "And no matter what, don't ask any questions. That's a dead giveaway. The very concept of a phrase in pursuit of new knowledge is so foreign to the programming of these people that it will immediately trigger the hive response. People who don't think are absolutely repulsed by questions."

"Got it," Richard replied. "No questions."

They stood at the edge of the forest and watched the villagers begin their day. There was an elderly woman selling eggs. A blacksmith lighting his furnace. A tiny man feeding something carrot-shaped to an equally tiny donkey. All gray, of course.

"See that well in the distance?" Rigot pointed to a small stone circle about knee-high with a gray wood top in the center of the village. "That's the extraction point."

"Very good," Lucifer said. "Let's go."

They crossed into the village and made a beeline for the well. As they walked, they were greeted by villagers.

"Good day," said a large woman carrying a basket of bread.

"Good day," Lucifer replied. He gave a courtly bow toward the woman and tipped an imaginary hat with his extended right hand.

"I feel like chicken tonight," the woman said.

"Lovely day for it," Lucifer replied.

"Hello," said a small boy with homemade crutches.

"Hi," Rigot said, as he waved to the boy.

"Variety is the spice of life!" the boy replied.

"I would love a pizza party," Rigot said.

The exchanges looked like fun, and Richard was eager for his turn. He figured he could say something about chimichangas or quote a fun catchphrase from one of his favorite movies.

"Fine day," said a large man in a butcher's apron.

"How're you?" Richard replied.

As soon as the words had escaped his lips, he realized he'd made a mistake. He had asked a question. Granted, it was a question that, when asked, no one really cared to answer accurately—a question most people treated as a meaningless greeting. Richard could think of thousands of times someone had greeted him with, "How're you?" and he had simply replied, "How're you?" in return, not even answering the question. But that didn't matter. It was a question.

Lucifer and Rigot stopped and stared at Richard, mouths agape.

The large man in the butcher's apron locked eyes on Richard and began marching toward him.

"The well!" Lucifer cried. "Run!"

The three dashed toward the center of the village.

The boy in crutches was now limping toward them at breakneck speeds. The woman had tossed her basket of bread and was in pursuit. They were joined by a town crier, a village idiot, and a priest—all lifeless in expression and beginning to form a ring around Richard and his companions.

"Split up!" Rigot shouted. "Force them to break up their clusters."

The three split up, Richard to the left, Rigot to the right, Lucifer sticking to the center path toward the well.

Lucifer reached the extraction point first but wasn't extracted. "Rigot! It isn't working!" He began running in circles around the well to prevent the villagers from clustering around him.

Rigot cut back toward the well, breaking through a loosely formed wall of villagers. He dashed toward Lucifer and grabbed his hand. As soon as they made contact, a green light appeared, and both men vanished.

Richard, trying to prevent the man in the butcher's apron from smothering him in a corner with his large abdomen, suddenly realized he was all alone. He managed to squeeze free, but the relief was short-lived. The villagers—all of them—were now solely focused on him.

He tried to make it to the extraction point, but the line of villagers had filled in between him and the well, creating an impenetrable barrier. They closed in around him, forming a cocoon of smelly, unbathed gray bodies, and began walking him toward the edge of the village.

"Lucifer! Rigot!" Richard shouted. "One! Get me out of h—!"

Suddenly, in a flash of green light, Richard found himself back in the caves of Mount Molay, where he was joined by Parataxis, Lucifer, and Rigot.

"Got him," One said, as Richard's eyes adjusted to the dimly lit cave.

"How are you?" Parataxis asked.

"Yeah, I get it," Richard replied. "I screwed up."

Parataxis, who had grown a red beard in their absence, frowned in confusion. "I do not know what you mean."

They had been gone for twelve hours in Ergonia—just over a month and a half in Hell—but aside from Parataxis's beard, everything was as they'd left it.

"He doesn't know what happened in Ergonia, my friend," Rigot said. "He was just being his pleasant self."

"Oh, sorry." Richard felt his face burn red with embarrassment.

Lucifer laughed. "My, aren't you a big one!" he said to Parataxis, looking him up and down. "Warrior, I assume? Rigot has always had a soft spot for warriors."

"Yes," Parataxis replied. "Warrior."

Now Rigot was the one turning red. "There isn't time for pleasantries, my friends. We need to go."

Lucifer placed a hand on Parataxis's shoulder. "I hate to ask this of you, especially since we only just met, but do you think you could guard these boxes a little longer? They're invaluable to me, and I don't have time to hide them."

"Yes. I will guard them." Parataxis straightened, eyes forward, visibly proud to be of service.

"Thank you," Lucifer said.

Richard exited the cave into blindingly bright daylight, accompanied by Lucifer and Rigot. The cold and dark Psychros had given way to a warm and breezy Anoixi. Under normal circumstances, it would have been a beautiful day in Hell. Unfortunately, the light only highlighted the relentless destruction.

Hell had been leveled. There were no trees. No flowers. No buildings. Just gray ash piled several feet high in drifts like snow. It looked like the surface of the moon except for the occasional smoldering embers and smoke emanating from the ground. The thick smell of smoke coated them as they stepped away from the cave entrance.

As he struggled to breathe, Richard felt a profound sense of loss. It wasn't quite grief but a hole in his understanding of reality. The loss ate away at his consciousness, and he sensed it could never be filled.

"Love what you've done with the place," Lucifer said. "Looks a bit different from how I left it, but I just can't put my finger on it."

Rigot gritted his teeth. "Maybe you shouldn't have left."

Richard wasn't touching the topic. He knew the pain behind their words.

When they arrived at the site of the former trampoline, they found it had been destroyed, leaving only a bent and blackened frame. A metallic chain ladder dangled from the sky.

A woman with a distant look in her eyes sat on one of the bottom rungs of the ladder and held the chains on both sides like it was a park swing, slowly moving it back and forth with her feet. Dressed in burnt and tattered clothing, she was thin and covered in soot, her face obscured by a layer of grime.

"Are you okay?" Richard asked.

"I've been better," the woman said. "If I'm being completely honest."

Richard recognized the voice. "Aster?"

"Yeah," she muttered. "Nice to see you both again." There was no smile this time. She seemed lost in thought. Politeness on autopilot.

"Aster, what happened here?" Richard asked. "Where is everyone?"

"Hiding," she faintly replied, without breaking her gaze into the distance. "Some in basements. Some in piles of rubble. In case GOD comes back."

"They left?"

"Yeah, three days ago. They were having fun tormenting us. Burning everything we built. Was worse than Old Hell."

"Where'd they go?"

Aster pointed a black soot-covered hand toward the top of the chain ladder. Toward the door. "There was a loud trumpet sound. It shook Hell like a quake. They all stopped and rushed back to this ladder. Left through the door. That was three days ago."

"Shouldn't you be hiding too?" Richard asked.

"I'm the lookout. In case they come back." Aster never broke her gaze from the horizon. She was in shock. Lost in her own memories of what had transpired.

Lucifer let go a muffled gasp—not of shock but anguish. "I'm so sorry, Aster," he said. "I never thought it would come to this. If I'd known, even for a second—"

Aster's face lit up upon recognizing the voice of her long-lost friend. She leapt off the chain ladder and rushed over to embrace him. "Lucifer! Is it really you?" She wrapped her arms around Lucifer's neck.

He embraced her, lifting her off the ground. "No, I'm just a guy who looks and sounds a lot like him. Richard and Rigot just bumped into me. Figured I was close enough."

"Shut up, asshole," Aster said.

The banter, reminiscent of the playful jokes Richard had shared with Clara, brought back memories for him. He knew that this was simply their way. The way she knew it was really him.

They released their embrace and stepped back, wiping tears from their eyes.

"Where have you been?" Aster asked.

"It's a long story," Lucifer answered. "Well, not really, I guess. I stole the ODO and AOD boxes. Went into the ODO dimension. Miscalculated the time dilation. Freed a bunch of people. These two pulled me out. That's about it."

"Ah, succinct." Aster nodded, with an expression of feigned understanding.

"Oh," Lucifer added, "I forgot to mention that there's a teapot heading toward Earth that emits pure entropy, and we need to stop it."

"That seems like a pretty important thing to have forgotten," Aster said.

"Yeah, sorry. Got ahead of myself there."

Richard was delighted to see Aster light up again but had grown anxious as he put the pieces together. The entropy emitter was no doubt related to the rushed call for the agents of GOD to return to headquarters. He imagined what Clara and their children might be experiencing in a world of absolute chaos. Earthquakes? Nuclear war? Roaming bands of flying pygmy giraffes that spewed sulfuric acid? The possibilities were terrifying.

He climbed onto the chain ladder. "I'm going up there. You coming, Aster?"

Aster glanced around and then looked Lucifer in the eyes.

He smiled and gazed up the ladder as if to say, "After you."

"Right behind you!" she shouted and started climbing the chain ladder behind Richard, followed closely by Lucifer and Rigot.

Chapter 24
All You Need Is Love

A fairly wise human once devoted his life to spreading the gospel of love and was subsequently killed for his words. This man taught that love was the single most important virtue. He taught that love was universal and knew no color, creed, or boundary. He taught that love could bring peace and harmony to the world. He taught that it was important to love one another over material things.

His name was John Lennon, and he was murdered by Mark David Chapman in December 1980 AD for, among other things, claiming his band, named for the misspelling of a small hard-shelled insect, was more popular than a gentleman named Jesus Christ.

Coincidentally enough, Mr. Christ was the second-best known historical figure to tout these same teachings two thousand years before Mr. Lennon. A modest carpenter, Mr. Christ spent the final years of his life as a sort of traveling magician, while touting the virtues of love. Like Mr. Lennon, Mr. Christ claimed love was the single most important rule for all of humanity to follow. And like Mr. Lennon, he was murdered for such a seemingly bizarre and unacceptable thought.

Following his death, a group adopted the habit of adorning their bodies and houses of worship with small replicas of the device used to torture and kill Mr. Christ. They also taught a dogma that, at times, seemed very much to contradict his central tenet of universal love. Ironically, they claimed to do so not to further denigrate the man but to spread his beliefs.

Even now, knowing in their heart of hearts this is true, cynics call love a bunch of trite gibberish. But it's easy to surrender to cynicism. It's much harder to actually love your fellow man . . .

———

I *should have stretched first*, a winded Richard thought as he neared the top of the chain ladder. He had been climbing for more than an hour. The bottoms of low-lying clouds were closer overhead than the surface of Hell was below, and his pace had slowed as he grew increasingly exhausted. He wrapped a bent arm around one rung of the ladder and paused to catch his breath.

That was the thing about climbing ladders into the sky. It was like dieting, exercise, and meditation. From the ground, it seemed so easy, so doable, and it wasn't until the halfway point that the climber realized the discomfort of reaching the top. By then, it was too late to back down.

"Come on, my friend, you can do this!" Rigot shouted. He was below Richard and Aster on the ladder but just ahead of Lucifer, who was bringing up the rear. He didn't sound the least bit winded. All of those morning workout sessions in the personal fitness section of the Biblio had clearly served him well.

"I know," Richard mumbled as he tried to swallow the taste of pennies. "I just . . . need . . . a minute." He wondered if letting go and hitting the ground thousands of feet below would be more or less painful than continuing on. They really didn't need him anyway, he thought. Surely, they could save Earth without what little value he brought to the table.

"Richard!" Lucifer shouted from below. "Inside every human is greatness. The ability to turn pain into something beautiful. It's part of who you are. I know you're in pain, but you need to channel that energy into saving Earth! You need to protect that little blue ball and all the beauty it represents!"

By now, Richard fully understood Lucifer's worldview—likely better than Lucifer understood it himself. "I know," he gasped. "I'm trying." He began to feel as though he could no longer hold on to the rung. The world around him felt unreal and seemed to move with a blurred lag.

"Fuck Dr. Gregg!" Aster shouted. "Fuck that guy! Richard, do you remember when you were ready to spend all of eternity resetting a box in your apartment for just a glance at your wife and kids?"

"Yeah," Richard said between gasps.

"It's all you wanted. All you cared about. You were consumed by grief. Obsessed. Richard, remember that obsession. That feeling that you would do anything for them. Fuck saving the world, and fuck beauty! Do it for them!"

Richard closed his eyes and all at once saw every moment of his time on Earth. The life flashing before his eyes he expected at death and never received. His first kiss with Clara. The day Tara was born. Family dinners. Moments where they broke each other's hearts and the subsequent apologies. Camping trips. Family road trips. Hide-and-seek in their back-yard. Each memory piled one upon the other, forming a mountain of sentimental moments that could have stretched from the surface of Hell to the door.

Richard stood atop the mountain and looked down, realizing the strength it took to climb it paled in comparison to the strength he would need to muster to make it to the top of the ladder. "Thanks, Aster," he said, as he grabbed hold of the ladder with both hands and began sprinting to the top, pushing through the pain and exhaustion.

Fifteen minutes later, he reached the door. Upon approach, he could see the door had been left open. He could see people running back and forth. He could hear people shouting and arguing. An occasional gust of office air conditioning would send sheets of white printer paper swirling through the opening.

Richard pulled himself into the doorway and crouched behind a large beige copy machine. He was soon joined by Aster, followed by Rigot and Lucifer.

The copy machine began printing off pages, making it impossible to communicate when combined with the sounds of pandemonium in the office.

Richard turned to Lucifer for instructions, but Lucifer, seemingly preoccupied, was eavesdropping on a conversation between a young man and a loud older redheaded woman at the water cooler a few yards from the copier. Being the nearest to the cooler, Richard joined Lucifer in attempting to discern the conversation between the two coworkers.

"I know," the woman said. "It's really awful. I mean, at this point, I'm just updating my resume in case we make it out of here."

The man she was speaking to responded in a normal volume and was thus too far away to be heard.

"Exactly," the woman replied. "When Joe's talking about applying for a permit to dump all life on Earth into the incinerator and start over, you know it has to be bad. I mean, sad for them, but what about us? Do we get terminated? Thrown into the incinerator as well? Or do we finally get to leave? I don't know about you, but the agreement I signed with my evaluator clearly said that upon termination, my only option was the incinerator, but that wouldn't apply here, would it?"

The man rambled on for much too long. His voice was still inaudible. Richard was pretty sure he'd made some tangent about musical identification and bleaching contacts, but that didn't make sense, given the context.

"Yeah, I guess," said the woman. "Well, it would be nice if Joe actually did something about it rather than sitting in his office feeling sorry for himself is all I'm saying. Our jobs are on the line, and he's having a pity party."

Richard turned to the others. "Joe's in his office. They're planning to dump Earth into Hell. We need to hurry."

"But how will we make it through without being seen?" Aster asked.

"I'll handle that." Lucifer stood, walked into the middle of the hallway, and raised his arms. "Ladies and gentlemen of GOD, can I have your attention?"

Only a few looked up from their desks or stopped panicking long enough to listen.

"For those of you who don't recognize me, I'm Lucifer. Maybe you've heard of me?"

The office fell silent.

"Well then," Lucifer said smugly, while surveying the workers' shocked faces, "I believe this is the part where someone here escorts me and my friends to Joe's office so we can end this shit show."

Richard, Aster, and Rigot stood up behind the copier, smirked, and waved awkwardly at the workers in the crowded office hallway.

"You!" Lucifer pointed to the loud woman at the water cooler. "You seem to know what's going on here. How about you escort us to Joe's office before you end up looking like her?" He pointed to a soot-covered Aster.

"I'm not . . . ," the woman muttered. "That'd get me into trouble."

"Oh, that ship's sailed, sweetheart," Lucifer said. "You think Joe's going to keep you around once Earth's wiped? Someone's in denial. Am I right?"

Richard, Aster, and Rigot nodded in agreement.

"And after you maniacs destroyed all the work we did in Hell, do you really think we're going to show any of you mercy? I've already asked Aster over here to remember your faces so the moment you land in Hell, we can begin your eternal torment."

Aster scrunched her nose and squinted her eyes and pretended to concentrate hard on the woman's face.

"So. Let's try this again. Escort me to Joe's office. *Now!*"

"Ri-right this way," stuttered the loud and trembling woman.

As she led them through GOD's corporate office, Richard got a feel for the overall sense of alarm in the building. Along with passing offices in which people were crying and screaming at one another, he had to dodge the occasional panicked worker dashing through the hallways. It felt like the end of the world was taking place within the walls of GOD headquarters itself.

In the stairwell, he found Peter, the evaluator, huddled in a corner of a landing and passionately kissing Janet, the woman from the DMV. In his off-white shirt and khaki pants, he looked like a thin tree branch supporting her tangerine body.

At least they're making their own kind of beauty from chaos, Richard thought.

After they reached the top floor, the loud woman held open

the stairway door, and they exited the stairway into an empty lobby with white marble walls and floors. A set of large mother-of-pearl doors featured the name *JOE* etched into them in big, bold letters. Below that was *CEO* in even larger and bolder letters.

"Okay, well, this is it. Good luck!" The loud woman slammed the stairway door behind her, and Richard could hear the echo of her rushed footsteps as she hurried down the stairs.

I can't believe that worked, Richard thought.

Rigot placed a hand on Lucifer's shoulder. "Well, my friend, after you."

Lucifer took a deep breath and pushed open the door to Joe's office. "I'm back, you son of a—" He froze, seemingly struck by the enormity of the room.

The room was dark. Thirty-foot-high ceilings loomed above wooden bookshelves that seemed to go on for the length of a football field. Black marble floors accented with a red Persian rug ran from the door to a gleam of light in the distance.

"Wow," Lucifer said, as he stared in wonderment at the room. "This looks nothing like the modest office Joe had during my last visit."

"Can I help you?" someone called out in a kindly old voice.

"Joe?" Lucifer shouted. "Is that you?"

There was no answer.

They jogged down the runner toward the gleam of light, and as the light gave way to shape and form, Richard could make out a large mahogany desk and a balding head of white hair resting atop black-suit-sleeved arms.

"Joe?" Lucifer said.

The man looked up. It was indeed Joe, but he didn't look like the cool, confident man from the video. He looked ill and sad. Red eyes, puffy from weeping. A sickly raspiness in his voice. "Here to kick me when I'm down, my old friend? Maybe steal something else from my company?"

"*Our* company," Lucifer said. "It was *our* company. You took it from me. I just took your abandoned project from a storage closet."

"You're a sore loser is what you are," Joe grumbled. "Lose a bet and steal the ante anyway. You've always been a snake."

"The only snakes here are the ones you fabricate to cover for your incompetence and greed," Lucifer snapped.

Rigot stepped between the two arguing men. "Yes, yes, my friends. Joe is controlling and greedy. Lucifer is sneaky and dishonest. Richard is a mediocre nobody. I'm a madman. And Aster . . ." He struggled to come up with a personality flaw. "Well, Aster's actually pretty great."

Aster nodded in agreement.

"Who's this joker?" Joe asked.

"This is my companion Rigot," Lucifer answered. "He's a real friend. He doesn't lie or change things behind my back after we agree on them. You know, like an honest person."

"Enough!" Richard said.

"Yeah, enough." Joe stood up to a hunch and hobbled over to the front of his desk. He sat on the edge, facing Lucifer at eye level. "You here to get the board to kick me out? Use this disaster to make some type of power play? If so, don't bother. You can have the damned thing. Take all of it."

"No," Lucifer replied. "I—"

"You know," Joe said, "when you get to my age, you start to take stock of your life. Why you did things a certain way. Why you didn't do others. All I ever wanted was love and respect. Just like anyone else. You create an entire dimension full of life. You give them free will—"

"*I* gave them free will," Lucifer said.

"Same difference," Joe replied. "The point is, all I ever

asked for in return was love and respect. Just as anyone else deserves. And now I have nothing." He wiped a red puffy eye with the back of a trembling hand.

"You never asked for love and respect," Lucifer said. "You *demanded* it. Anyone who didn't give it to you was thrown into an incinerator. You're controlling. How could anyone love someone who thought so little of them that he would throw them away like trash? You confuse fear with respect. You're not the victim here. *They* are." He pointed to Richard and Rigot.

"They're humans?" Joe asked, with a quizzical look.

"Yes," Lucifer replied. "Look, I know how to stop this. I still can if you'll let me."

"Why bother?" Joe said. "Do you think anyone is going to pay for the results of a simulation with a big chaos-sized hole in its timeline? Even if we fix it now, it'll be worthless. Might as well just wait for the trajectory modification permit approval and then dump the whole thing into the incinerator."

Joe's words sent a chill down Richard's spine. He was filled with disgust and anger. "And they call me a nobody," he muttered.

"Excuse me?" Joe said.

"I said, I can't believe they call me a nobody. In what reality am I a nobody and you a somebody?"

"Now you listen here," Joe said, pointing a finger at Richard in anger.

"No," Richard shot back. "*You* listen. Do you want to know why you could never get someone to really love you? Why you couldn't get people to truly respect you? Because you're a fool if you think that's how it works."

"Richard," Rigot said, "this might not be the best time—"

"Not now, Rigot," Richard said, still staring at Joe. "You don't command love. You don't demand respect. You give it, and it comes back to you tenfold. Back on Earth, I may not have been rich or successful or had a lot of fancy things, but I did have love and respect. I never demanded it. I *earned* it. I respected my wife, and she respected me in return. I loved my family and gave them everything. I gave them my dreams. I gave them my time. You could even say I gave them my life. And if I had to do it again, I would, because I love them."

Joe was silent.

Richard looked at Lucifer. "A wise man once told me that the only reason anyone cares to be somebody is so that others love and validate them." He looked back at Joe. "You're the ultimate somebody, and still you missed the point. Love isn't some zero-sum resource you can demand others give to you. You start by loving others, and that starts by having a little damned empathy. Actually caring about someone other than yourself." Richard took a deep breath to calm himself. "I just . . . I don't know how you watch the entirety of human history and completely miss such an obvious message. You'd have to be blind."

A calm fell upon the room as everyone looked around, not knowing what to say next.

Everyone, that was, everyone except Joe, who was staring down at his shoes in thought, arms locked across his chest. "You know," Joe said, "it's been a long time since someone spoke to me that way. I always assumed humans were just incapable of it. But, it . . . it's the fear, isn't it? People aren't honest with me because they're afraid."

"Well, my friend," Rigot said, "you do threaten to throw people into an incinerator."

Joe chuckled. "Fair enough. Maybe you're right, Raymond."

"It's Richard."

"Ah, yes, Richard. Sorry. Maybe you're right. Maybe I'm the one that's broken. Maybe I deserve the incinerator."

"No one deserves that," Richard said. "That's the point. You aren't perfect. None of us are. Well, except maybe for Aster."

Aster again nodded with a smile.

Joe turned to Lucifer. "We did pretty good with these humans, huh?"

"Yes, we did," Lucifer said.

"A lot of that was you," Joe said. "I mean, I helped. The whole appendix thing and wisdom teeth were some of my better ideas. But really, we nailed it with these things."

Lucifer smiled. "We made a good team."

"I'm sorry, my old friend," Joe said.

"Yeah, me too," Lucifer replied.

The moment was broken by a loud wailing. It was Rigot, consumed by emotion. "That was so beautiful, my friends." He gave Lucifer and Joe an enormous hug that lasted an awkwardly long time.

Joe finally broke free of the embrace and scurried back behind his desk. He opened the center drawer and pulled out a blue lanyard with a gray key card attached to the end. He turned to Lucifer with wild, energetic eyes, "Let's fix this."

Chapter 25
Snake Shit

Joe used a cane and shuffled his feet as he led Richard and his companions down the flickering, fluorescent-light-bathed hallways of the GOD corporate offices. "Almost there. I think you'll find we've done some upgrades to the control room since you were last here."

"Oh?" Lucifer said.

"Yeah, big and flashy. No real difference in functionality, but clients love this kind of showy high-tech mumbo jumbo. Take them on a tour, and it's all 'Ooh!' and 'Aah!' Makes them whip out the checkbooks." He winked at Lucifer.

"You always had a gift for showmanship," Lucifer replied.

"Showmanship is salesmanship," Joe said, pounding the floor with the end of his cane with enthusiasm. "And salesmanship keeps this ship afloat." He held up his key card and opened a set of plain white office doors. "Anyway, the control room is right through here."

The doors opened to a massive circular room with a towering domed ceiling. The walls were lined with stacked columns of concrete platforms, each containing rows of gray metal desks surrounded by monitors projecting scenes from life on Earth. The room was filled with workers in business casual attire scurrying about, trying to figure out what had gone wrong with the simulation. In the center of the room was a large white pillar that jetted up hundreds of feet from the ground into the vertical center of the room. Atop this pillar sat a small metal box, the size of a pizza box, with black wires running from it in all directions.

"Wow," Lucifer said. "You weren't kidding about the upgrade. I remember when we had that thing sitting on a folding table near the break room."

"The good ol' days," Joe said, with a smile.

He walked up to a workstation where a large, disheveled, and sweaty-looking man sat, hunched over his keyboard, locked in a trance with his monitor.

"Any luck?" Joe asked, startling the man.

"Oh! It's . . . Hi! Um, I'm sorry. I'm just working on . . . I can't seem to get it to . . . But I can't find . . . I, I, I . . ." The man hung his head in defeat. "I'm sorry. Please don't fire me."

Joe rolled his eyes, "Stop groveling, big fella. Go take a break. We just need your terminal." He pointed his cane toward the door.

"Right," the man said, trembling. He stood up from his desk chair, grabbed a small paper bag from his desk, and scurried away.

Joe turned to Lucifer. "It's all yours."

Lucifer took a seat at the terminal and pulled up a command line of green text in a black window. "To find the teapot, we just need to find the point of highest concentrated entrophy." He began entering a series of commands into the terminal.

"Teapot?" Joe asked.

"Yeah, a teapot," Lucifer replied, eyes still locked on the

terminal screen. "I added it back when I added that tree to the garden. It emits entropy. Keeps things a little chaotic."

"A little chaotic." Joe shook his head in disbelief. *"That's* why we never seemed to have control. We've been trying to solve that entropy anomaly for millennia. Always seemed like an intermittent issue. By the time we'd get close to figuring it out, it'd seem to disappear on its own. Like chasing a ghost."

"By design," Lucifer said. "It wasn't on Earth until you destroyed Hell and the device that kept it in orbit. So I like to think of this mess as your fault."

"How was I to know you were going to put some kind of entrophy teacup in space?"

"Teapot," Lucifer replied. "It's a teapot. And I've just about tracked down its location." He brought up a map on the terminal screen with a red dot seemingly sitting in the middle of the Pacific Ocean.

"Zoom in," Joe said.

Lucifer hit a few keys on the keyboard, and the map zoomed in. The dot that previously appeared to be floating in the middle of the ocean was now situated over an extremely small island. A few pixels of green in an ocean of blue.

"I knew it!" Joe said. "Babadooshuru! Half the planet's pinkeye outbreaks come from missionaries sent to that one tiny island. The natives think they're living snake shit or something like that. Humans."

"Still can't control 'em, huh?" Lucifer replied.

Joe laughed. "Not like I don't try. They really seem to enjoy making me bonkers, you know? Sent Josh from human resources down there a few millennia ago as our representative. Told them to just try and be a little nicer to one another. That didn't seem to go over well at all. Somehow, it made it worse. Poor guy still shudders whenever he writes a lowercase letter *t*."

Staring at images of Earth, Richard grew increasingly anxious. "So what do we do now?"

"Well," Lucifer said, "since I made the teapot uncontrollable from here, we have two options. Option one: we send a giant meteor to destroy the entire island, killing all of the inhabitants and potentially starting a short period of global winter but saving Earth in the long run."

"And option two?" Richard asked, not caring for option one.

"We could send a search party down there. I'm thinking, you, Aster, and Rigot. I'd have to stay here and handle the terminal. You three would have to find the teapot and destroy it."

"I say we go for option two," Richard said.

"I'm up for it," Aster added.

"I agree, my friends," Rigot said. "Seems less . . . *genocidal*." He turned to Joe. "Sorry. I don't mean to judge."

"It's quite all ri—"

Before Joe could finish his sentence, Lucifer entered a few keystrokes, and a bright white light shot from the box sitting atop the pillar in the center of the room, striking the search party and sending them to the island of Babadooshuru.

Richard found himself in the midst of a sandy clearing, encircled by swaying palm trees. Within the clearing stood numerous bamboo huts and communal buildings, all covered with palm-thatched roofs. At first glance, the place resembled a tropical paradise—aside from the pea-green sky that was dropping a deluge of frogs like rain.

"I think this must be the right place, my friends," Rigot said, as he swatted away a large bullfrog that had landed on his shoulder.

"Ya think?" A cowering Aster tried to cover her face against the slimy onslaught of falling leopard, horned, and glass frogs.

196

"The hut!" Richard pointed to the nearest open-air pavilion. "Over there!"

The three sprinted toward the hut and took refuge inside. They were not alone. Sheltering inside were dozens of Babadooshians, clothed only in red loincloths and palm-thatched vests, all in a panic caused by the ominously amphibious weather. They were coping the only way they knew how: by taking turns wallowing in a pile of serpent feces in an attempt to appease the great snake god.

"So," Aster said, "now what?"

"My friends," Rigot said, "the way I see it, there's little chance the teapot landed on the island without shattering. That would lead me to believe it landed in the ocean and washed ashore here."

"Excellent point," Richard said. "So we should probably head toward the shore."

"But which one?" Aster asked. "It's an island. It's nothing but shore."

A loud rumbling in the nearby palm forest stole Richard's attention. He could see the tops of palms disappear over the horizon, accompanied by loud crashes as each hit the ground. A moment later, an enormous red seven-headed dragon broke through the tree line, sending bits of palm fronds and splinters flying through the air. The dragon had large steely scales and was the size of a camper van. Each of its seven heads had a pair of black eyes—fourteen in total. Among the seven heads were ten horns, which made the creature disturbingly asymmetrical. A bit odd-looking, Richard thought, but terrifying, nonetheless.

"Damnit!" said the third dragon head in a deep, rumbling voice. "I knew we were lost!"

"Now, hon," said the fourth head in a woman's voice that resembled that of a sweet southern socialite, "there's no reason to go panickin'. We just got here. Just gotta keep a cool head is all."

"But I'm hungry!" shouted the seventh head in a child's voice.

"Me too!" shouted heads one and two, joined by the rest.

"I swear to Draco!" said the third head, "if one more person complains about being hungry, we're just going to turn around and go home."

"Language, David," whispered the fourth head. "Don't lose your cool. This whole vacation was your idea, hon, remember?"

"Don't start with me, Irene," said David, the third head. "This was supposed to be a fun trip. Some cave guarding. Some jewel hoarding. Maybe an evening of fire breathing. Now we're stuck on some tiny island in the middle of nowhere, all of our food options are covered in serpent shit, and now it's raining fucking frogs. How do you think that makes me feel as a husband and father? As a provider?"

"I know, hon," Irene said, with a reassuring tone. "But we don't think any less of you, do we, kids?"

"No," the remaining five heads said in unison.

"Well, maybe a little," said head six.

"Thanks, everyone," David said. "It's just hard, you know? Being somewhere new. Trying to have a good time. Relieve some stress. And now all this. It's a lot of pressure. I just wanted everyone to have a good time. Some nice family bonding, you know?"

"We love you, Dad," said head number five. "We'll figure this out."

"Together," Irene said. "We'll figure this out *together*."

The dragon picked up speed and dashed through the village, destroying several small huts and making a new opening in the palm forest on the opposite side of the clearing.

Somehow, it was the first thing since his death that made

Richard feel less homesick, but he didn't have the time to delve into those emotions. "Well," he said, "that was somewhat anti-climactic. Big red dragon, and it doesn't even try to eat us?"

"Are you disappointed, my friend?" Rigot asked.

"No, of course not. It's just . . ." Richard decided it would be best to change the subject. "I'm guessing our best bet is to follow that trail of destruction back to wherever whatever-that-was came from."

Each grabbed a palm frond from the dragon's trail of destruction, using them as protection against the falling frogs, and followed the trail toward shore.

As they walked the freshly cleared path to the shore, Richard heard thunderous humming in the distance.

"What do you think that noise is?" Aster asked.

"It could be pink paisley clams that shoot pepper sauce, for all we know," Rigot replied. "From what Lucifer's told me of chaos, I imagine this type of concentrated entrophy can produce random mutations in reality beyond what we can comprehend."

"Beyond what we can comprehend?" Richard chuckled. "And your first thought was paisley clams shooting sauce?"

"Look, my friend," Rigot said, with an embarrassed smile, "you try coming up with random combinations of unimaginable things and let me know how well you do. I've told you before: a mind can't come up with all the variations that chaos can create."

As they approached the shore, the surroundings took on an increasingly peculiar appearance. Initially resembling palm trees, the vegetation soon transformed into what seemed like banana trees, which wasn't all that strange, Richard thought, and could have just as easily been a form of agriculture by the Babadooshians. But the strangeness escalated when, just a few feet away, the banana trees morphed into colossal thirty-foot bananas protruding from the sand. As they moved a few yards farther, the setting evolved into a terrain of burnt-orange shag carpet with bushes of Vienna sausages scattered amid a forest of massive walnut coat racks with opossums affixed to the tops by their tails. The opossums screeched and swung erratically to maneuver toward the sausage bushes.

"I think it's safe to assume we're heading in the right direction," Richard said.

When they reached the seashore, there was no question as to the location of the teapot. The beach was made of a variety of jagged children's toys. Small plastic building bricks, broken action figures, marbles, small toy cars with missing wheels—all piled into mounds like dunes of sand. The ocean itself was a never-ending pile of wrinkled laundry, washed and dried but not yet folded. The tide of laundry came in and withdrew from the piles of toys like waves. Absolute chaos of the highest magnitude.

One hundred yards down the beach, just a few feet from the edge of the laundry pile, a fluffy white marshmallow the size of a small cottage hovered above an aquamarine abyss that was vomiting all manner of strange creatures and objects onto its periphery. A giant duck eating lamb and a giant duck-eating lamb. Gerbils riding toasters. Ducks in turtle pants and turtles in duck pants. Anthropomorphic alligators in neon pink workout leotards and purple sweatbands. One horse-sized duck and one hundred duck-sized horses. Entrophy seemed to have a thing for ducks, which should make sense to anyone who understands the nature of ducks.

Atop the marshmallow sat a red teapot. Nothing too showy or impressive. The kind Richard could imagine spotting at a local discount or thrift store. Cheap and utilitarian.

"There it is!" Aster shouted, pointing to the teapot.

The three ran in the direction of the teapot, giving no consideration to the developing chaos around it.

"We just need to get close enough to strike it," Rigot said. "We can figure out how to cross the abyss once we get there."

Aster and Rigot raced ahead, running with a comfortable stride, but Richard lagged one hundred feet behind, winded and gasping for air.

"Hurry, my friend!" Rigot shouted. "We're so close!"

"I know," a panting Richard said. He watched as Aster and Rigot's lead widened. He felt awful—not just physically but emotionally. He was slowing them down. Bringing down the team with his mediocrity. And then . . .

"No!" Aster yelled.

"Damnit!" howled Rigot.

From Richard's vantage point, he could see them sinking into the ground, their legs and lower torsos submerged below the piles of toys.

He ran as quickly as he could. When he caught up to his friends, they were yelling and cursing, their lower bodies stuck below the surface of a tide pool made of a sticky pink substance like used chewing gum.

"I'm sorry, my friend," Rigot said. "I thought it was solid."

"Me too," Aster said. "Chewing gum quicksand doesn't exactly register on my mental list of things to look out for."

"I get it," Richard said, trying to catch his breath. "Let me see if I can pull you out."

Richard knelt down, grabbed Aster by the one hand she hadn't already accidentally submerged into the gum, and attempted to pull her out from the edge of the pool, but it was fruitless. She was stuck.

"You'll have to do this alone, my friend," Rigot said.

As Richard glanced toward the teapot, now less than fifty feet away, a creature resembling a lion with six wings and a human face was retched from the abyss. Its skin was covered in eyeballs, except for its face, which had only the customary two.

"Ouch! Ouch! Ouch! Son of a bitch!" the creature wailed from its human mouth as the eyeballs at the bottoms of its feet came in contact with the surface of jagged and broken children's toys. "Why? Why was I created this way? Gah! Dammit!" The creature tried to shift its weight back and forth on its eyeball-covered feet, not realizing it had wings. It was unable to rest its weight on a body part without rubbing it against an open eyeball. "I mean, gah! I get the benefit of more eyeballs. Ouch! But why the feet? Why the feet?" It fell onto its side, striking even more of the eyeballs on the piles of toys, howled in excruciating pain, and then rolled into the ocean of laundry, where it finally found some relief.

"Um," Aster said, "that was pretty messed up."

"Yeah," Rigot replied, still in a state of shock.

They both looked back at Richard.

"I'm supposed to single-handedly fight that kind of chaos?"

"Yes," Rigot said. "Remember, my friend, chaos is the name we give to random chance when it doesn't go our way."

"I'm not sure how that's supposed to help," Richard replied, "but thanks, I guess."

"It's not malicious. It has no ill intent toward you. It's random. Despite its power, the teapot shouldn't try to stop you. You just have to contend with reaching it in spite of any undirected chaos it produces."

"Just remember," Aster added, "it may hurt, but you can't avoid the pain of chaos. All you can do is keep moving forward."

Richard stood up from the edge of the gum pool and again stared at the teapot. "Not like I can die again, right?"

"That's the spirit!" exclaimed Aster.

Richard jogged toward the teapot, quickly reaching the

edge of the void. He stared into the abyss, but it didn't stare back, because it was just an abyss and not sentient in any way.

The abyss was thirty feet wide from end to end. Its aquamarine pool of light spun in a gyre, emitting an unsettling aura at its edge.

The marshmallow that floated just a few feet above the abyss's center was fourteen feet wide and twenty feet tall. To reach the teapot, Richard would need to clear the eight-foot gap to the marshmallow and then grab onto the edge of the marshmallow and climb on top. Failure in any way meant falling into an ocean of pure entropy.

I need something long and light, he thought. *Something I can use to pull myself to the top of the marshmallow.*

That was when he had his epiphany. He could make a rope from the sea of unfolded laundry, tie the end to a heavy and jagged broken toy, and toss the toy to the top of the marshmallow, knocking the teapot into the abyss. If he missed, he could still hope to embed the toy into the top of the marshmallow, allowing him to pull himself to the top. It was the perfect plan.

Richard rushed over to the ocean of laundry and began picking through it for sturdy long-sleeved articles that could be tied together easily. As he grabbed a long tan jacket, he found beneath it the winged eyeball creature with the human face.

"Please, kill me," pleaded the creature as it wallowed in pain. "My existence is agony."

"You know you can fly, right?" Richard said. "I'm not telling you how to live your life, but that does seem slightly better than wallowing in torment."

"I . . . I can?" asked the creature.

"I would assume so," Richard replied. "You have six wings. That has to mean something, right?"

"I do?"

"Yeah, you do. Maybe try flapping them rather than focusing on how badly your eyes hurt."

The creature began flapping its wings. At first the effort was sloppy and unproductive, but it kept trying until it began to rise from the ground. Within seconds it was flying through the air and hovering above the ocean of laundry.

"Hey!" the creature shouted. "Look at me! I'm flying!"

"Great job!" Richard shouted.

"Everything's so beautiful from up here! I can see all of it from every angle! This is why I have eyes on my feet!"

"That's great!" Richard shouted, trying to be encouraging. Richard had a new plan. "Hey, do you think you could give me a lift? Drop me on top of that giant marshmallow over there?"

"Absolutely!" shouted the creature, as it swooped down and grabbed Richard in its eyeball-coated hands. "Ouch!" shouted the creature. "Okay, so the eyeball contact still hurts a lot, but let's get you dropped off."

"Sorry!" Richard said, as they reached the top of the marshmallow.

The creature released Richard, dropping him toward the surface of the marshmallow. As he fell, the teapot grew closer. The nightmare was almost over. He could feel it.

But when Richard approached the marshmallow's surface, an enormous burrito emerged unexpectedly. The burrito, which had a baboon's face on one end and a sizable red rear end on the other, soared through the air with a wide-eyed, terrified expression. Propelled by spewing refried beans, it emitted a loud, piercing screech as it collided with Richard midair. The impact knocked Richard off course, sending him crashing onto the sharp plastic ladder of a toy fire engine at the edge of the abyss.

It's not personal, Richard assured himself. *It's undirected chaos. That's just the way things go sometimes.*

He stood up and limped to the edge of the ocean of laundry again in an attempt to salvage his original plan. After gathering enough clothing to make the rope he needed, he headed back to shore, aching and defeated but not without hope.

He sat on the ground near the edge of the abyss and began tying the sleeves of the garments together. When he was done, he set out to find a toy that could serve as a makeshift grappling hook.

"That was a nasty spill back there, my friend!" Rigot shouted from the gum pool. "But do you think you could hurry it up a bit?"

"I'm trying!" Richard snapped. "Just give me a minute."

He bent down to pick up the fire engine he had landed on earlier, convinced of both its sturdiness and sharpness, and tied it to the end of the laundry rope. Then he swung the engine in a circle above his head, building momentum with each rotation. When he released the rope, the fire engine flew through the air, struck the marshmallow on its side near the top, and fell short of its target.

Richard pulled it back toward himself to try again. *Keep moving forward,* he thought. *Never give up.*

As he swung the engine for another attempt, he heard a thunderous humming sound—the same one he had heard earlier. It grew louder until it was almost deafening. Richard shrugged it off. He would not be stopped by whatever new chaos this was.

At the moment he was ready to release the rope, he heard an angry voice in his left ear.

"Whaddya think you're doin'?"

Richard stopped and looked around but saw no one.

"Hey! Prick! Over here! On ya shoulder!"

Richard glanced at his left shoulder and saw perched atop it a single locust with a man's face, long flowing hair, sharp teeth, and the tail of a scorpion. He gasped and instinctively swatted at the creature with his right hand, knocking it to the ground.

"Oh, I see how it is," said the locust as it rolled over and stood on the foot of a disembodied action figure leg. "First ya go messin' with my fire engine, and now ya hit me? Well, buddy, you don't know who you're messin' with."

"No," Richard said. "I'm sorry. It's just that—"

From the opening in the toy pile made from the removal of the fire engine flew thousands of human-faced locusts with scorpion tails. They swarmed around Richard and stung him relentlessly, sending him into a dark tunnel of agony.

He tried to remain calm and block out the pain. *It's not personal*, he assured himself. *This too will pass. Take the pain and move forward.*

The swarm of locusts then latched themselves onto his clothing and skin and lifted him into the air.

"Let's see how you like being smacked to the ground!" shouted the original locust.

Richard continued to ascend into the sky while in the grasp of the swarm, all the while being stung and called all manner of vulgar things by the locusts.

I know it's not personal, but this sure feels personal, Richard thought, as he internalized his suffering. *Extremely personal.*

Finally, hovering thousands of feet in the air, the swarm released Richard, sending him plummeting toward the jagged surface below.

The sensation of falling was familiar. He remembered the last time he'd felt it, when he had been thrown into Hell. The fear and turmoil. The feeling of his clothes whipping in the wind. The sense of the injustice of it all. A good man, trying to do the right thing, cheated by an uncaring universe.

Like the last time, he closed his eyes and thought of his

family and how much he missed them. He reminded himself that no matter how much it hurt, he would have to get back up and keep going—for them.

And, just like the last time, his thoughts were interrupted when he hit something surprisingly soft and bounced back into the air.

"What the . . . ," he muttered to himself.

He opened his eyes and found himself lying atop the marshmallow, the teapot within arm's length.

Marshaling what little strength he had left, Richard lifted his heavy, throbbing arm into the air and maneuvered it toward the teapot. He dropped it like a dead weight just inches from the teapot handle, and as he tried to grab the teapot, he realized his fingers were swollen and unusable. The locusts' venom had diminished his fine motor function. He couldn't move a single swollen digit.

Delirious from pain and inebriated from poison, he began to cackle and howl like a drunk. "Oh! This would be my luck!" he screamed as he lay on his back staring into the sky. "Undirected chaos, right? Random, right? Rains on the just and the unjust, right? It sure seems to rain wherever I go!" Then, as most drunks do after one too many, he began to sing. "'You work and work for years and years, you're always on the go! You never take a minute off, too busy makin' dough! Someday, you say, you'll have your fun, when you're a millionaire! Imagine all the fun you'll have in your old rockin' chair!'"

It was the last song he'd heard before his death, the song Clara had sung in the kitchen on his last night on Earth.

"'Enjoy yourself, it's later than you think! Enjoy yourself, while you're still in the pink! The years go by, as quickly as you wink! Enjoy yourself, enjoy yourself, it's later than you think!'"

He could hear Clara singing it with him. In his mind they were together in the kitchen. She was dancing in her floral robe.

They were happy. Then she suddenly began to fade away, back into a distant memory. Richard frantically reached to grab her hand as she drifted away, but instead of the warmth of her touch, he found something cold and smooth.

Her image faded away, and Richard found himself inexplicably gripping the handle of the teapot. He lifted it into the air and, with his last remaining strength, smashed it against his swollen knee, shattering it.

Overcome by the pain and bodily trauma, he blacked out.

Chapter 26
Forty Years Later

M ost religions tell stories of individuals punished for acts of selflessness.

The ancient Greeks had Prometheus, who stole fire from the gods and gave it to humanity in the form of knowledge and technology. He was tied to a rock by Zeus and forced to have his liver eaten by an eagle each morning for breakfast.

The Christians have Mr. Christ, who taught a lesson of love and acceptance. He was tortured and killed.

The Babadooshians have the heroine Kerontica, who brought them the milk of the great snake (the coconut). She was cursed with a headache at the sight of a naked man.

As they say, seldom does a good deed go unpunished. But these stories also show that those who do good find solace in the end. Mr. Christ arose from the grave. Prometheus was freed by Hercules. Kerontica had the ideal excuse to rebuff the advances of her boorish husband, Nunnilingus.

In the end, these stories teach that those who put the good of others before their own self-interest ultimately win. This story is no different . . .

———

R ichard chuckled as he pretended not to notice the gawkers trying to sneak a peek at him through the aisles at New Gehenna Grocery.

He had no need for groceries, just as he had no need to eat. But he understood the importance of finding joy and pleasure in his meaningless existence, no matter how fleeting.

The gawkers weren't there to buy groceries but to catch a glimpse of the man who had saved Hell and Earth. The man who had changed the heart of GOD itself. The man who had helped lead the rebuilding of New Gehenna.

Much to their surprise, he wasn't much to look at. In fact, he looked like an exceptionally unexceptional man of average height and weight, middle-aged, and exactly a five on the standard one-to-ten scale of attractiveness based on the opinions of the opposite sex and a small number of the same sex who had given his appearance any consideration at all.

He was all of those things. The most nobody of nobodies and somebody of somebodies. But today, he was just a man looking for something quick and easy for dinner.

He waved at the gawkers as he left the grocery. He always took pleasure in their shock and sincere embarrassment.

Forty Earth years had passed since Richard had broken the teapot. Forty years of lasting friendship with Rigot, Lucifer, Aster, and Parataxis.

Rigot and Lucifer were closer than ever. Roommates—and perhaps more—they were inseparable. They shared a cottage in the countryside outside of New Gehenna where they would while away their days tinkering, baking, arguing over their philosophical differences, and preparing for their annual trip to Ergonia to check on the progress of the ongoing emancipation.

They had eternity to make up for lost time and planned to use every second of it.

Aster had been offered Lucifer's former role as Ruler of Hell but had turned it down in favor of rebuilding the democratic system that existed before the Day of Destruction. She now served as the elected Speaker of the Hell Caucus, assuring a fair and kind government for all.

Parataxis had hit it big with his bestselling book of poetry entitled, *How Are You?* His works explored the fundamental nature of existence and its impact on someone's emotional state. He continued to work as Parataxis the Pleasant Published Poet and had a wing at the new Belial Biblio named in his honor.

After the close call with Earth, Joe retired to Florida. He wished he'd done it years earlier.

As Richard walked to his apartment carrying his armful of groceries, he took in a deep breath of the cool Hell air, which filled his lungs and gave him a sense of calm. He was living his best life, or dying his best death, however he chose to look at it.

When he arrived at his apartment door, he reached into his pocket in search of his keys, while balancing the brown paper bag full of groceries on one knee. Just as he thought he was about to successfully execute the maneuver, he fumbled the bag, spilling its contents on the hallway floor.

He dropped to his hands and knees and crawled across the hallway floor, picking up the spilled groceries and placing them back into the bag he dragged behind him in one hand. It was a look unbecoming of the greatest hero in Hell.

As he crawled toward a can of spaghetti that had rolled to the other end of the hallway, he was stopped by the familiar voice of a woman standing in the nearby open elevator.

She laughed adoringly at his ridiculousness. "Five-minute rule, right?"